The Girl
from Cardigan

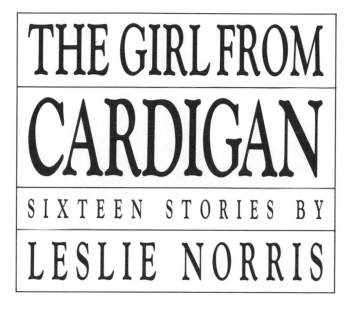

THE GIRL FROM
CARDIGAN

SIXTEEN STORIES BY

LESLIE NORRIS

GIBBS M. SMITH, INC.
Peregrine Smith Books
Salt Lake City

First paperback printing

93 92 91 90 89   5 4 3 2 1

Copyright © 1988 by Leslie Norris

This is a Peregrine Smith Book; published by Gibbs Smith, Publisher, P.O. Box 667, Layton, Utah 84041

Design by J. Scott Knudsen

On the cover: *Farm, Cardiganshire,* (1983), painting by John Elwyn; used with permission of Keith Walker, Wichester

Manufactured in the United States of America

Library of Congress Cataloging-in-Publication Data
Norris, Leslie, 1921-
    The girl from Cardigan : sixteen stories / by Leslie Norris.
        p.   cm.
    ISBN 0-87905-337-2
    I. Title.
PR6027.O44G5   1989   89-4035
823′.914—dc20   CIP

The paper used in this publication meets the minimum requirements of American National Standard for Information Sciences—Permanence of paper for Printed Library Materials, ANSI Z39.48-1984 ∞

Table of Contents

Acknowledgements

"The Girl from Cardigan," "A Flight of Geese," "The Kingfisher," "In the West Country" and "Lurchers" were first published in the *New Yorker*.

"My Uncle's Story," "Shaving" and "Sing It Again, Wordsworth" appeared in the *Atlantic Monthly*.

"The Wind, The Cold Wind," was published in the *Missouri Review*.

"Gamblers," "The Holm Oak" and "A Piece of Archangel" appeared in *Shenandoah*.

"Blackberries" was published in *BYU Today*.

For Kitty

The Girl
From Cardigan

I was never exactly a cuckoo in the nest, since there was no chance of pushing anyone out of our house, large and demanding though I was. My grandmother and my mother were small and unyielding; their hardness was a prime fact of life: their elbows and hands were hard, their words were quiet and hard, hardest of all was the judgment of their eyes. I was, no doubt of it, idle, clumsy, without any promise at all. There were just the three of us. My father made his escape when I was a baby. I can't remember anything about him.

I went once to Francis Nolan's house, years ago, when I was about thirteen. "Selwyn Howard? You're George Howard's boy," Francis' dad said.

"How do you know?" I said. I hoped it was because I looked like my father, could claim resemblance to somebody. I certainly didn't look like the two dapper women in our house. But Francis' dad only laughed. I used to see him about. Years later he told me my father lived in Birmingham and was very happy.

Our house was filled with small, convoluted, and brittle objects. I only had to turn around and five or six of them lay broken on the carpet—fragile china baskets of china flowers, winsome breakable dogs with tails that snapped at a glance. It didn't matter how many I broke. My grandmother replaced them at once from some inexhaustible store. She would take the dustpan and brush, remove the shards of my passage, sneer audibly at my great feet. As best I could, I would slink away. Slinking was difficult for me.

We lived in a small town in Monmouthshire, at the head of one of the coal valleys. Unemployment was endemic there, and enforced leisure gave rise to protracted bouts of philosophy and politics. Most men leaned toward politics, since it gave an appearance of energy and deceived some people into believing they possessed power and influence. It was, if you like, political theory, imaginative and vituperative. The hills about our town were full of men giving their views an airing; eloquence was commonplace.

True power lay in the hands of a small group—the aldermen and councillors of the town. To a man, they sold insurance and were prosperous. This was because they ran the municipal transport, the public parks and gardens, the collection of taxes, the whole organization of local government in the town and its surrounding villages. They hired and fired, dispensed and took away. They were so corrupt that the Mafia never got a toehold among us. Those Italian boys would have starved.

In order to get anywhere in our town you had to buy insurance. When teachers, for example, got their salaries at the end of the month, most of them paid heavy insurance. The remainder of the teachers were the sons and daughters of councillors.

One day my mother and I were walking together down Wallhead Road. She was explaining to me that as I was eighteen it was time I found gainful employment and that no gentleman walked as I walked, his toes turned in, his knees bent, his arms hanging apelike at his sides, his expression vacant, his very being a shame and burden. No family, she continued, had been so vexed. "And, talking of family, there's my cousin."

Her cousin, Harvey Lockwood, was one of the councillors. His insurance business was reputed to be the richest in the county, his daughters, all three, taught in the best schools, his house was full of antiques and carpets. I had seen him smoking a cigar—symbol of incredible wealth. We had never been in his house. We were the poor relations. Seeing us, he thought to avoid us by crossing the street, but the traffic was not kind to him. My mother planted herself in front of him. For a moment, I thought he would knock her down, so steadfastly was he looking at something above her head.

"Good morning," she said to Harvey. It was a nice morning, in fact, but winter was in her eye.

Harvey's start was a pleasant mixture of simulated surprise and delight. "Elsie," he said.

"You remember my name!" said my mother. "That's amazing." She said it cynically, and with reproof.

"Now, Else," said Harvey. "There's no need for sarcasm. After all, we're family. Our mothers were sisters, after all."

I noticed that he had begun to wriggle and turn red. There was no cure for this, as I knew. My mother examined coldly the growing evidence of Harvey's embarrassment.

"And who is this?" he blustered. "This young man can't be your Selwyn? What a size he's grown!"

"Hullo, Mr. Lockwood," I said nastily.

"Oh, Uncle Harvey," he said. "Call me Uncle Harvey." He turned to my mother. "Now that I look at him," he said, "he has a look of his grandfather about him. What a handsome fellow the old man was! What a big man! Pity he had such expensive habits."

"That's a nice coat you're wearing, Harvey," my mother said. "And where's that lovely new car of yours?" Harvey winced. I could have told him he had no chance. "When are you and Sylvia going to Paris again?" my mother said, turning the steel.

"What are you going to do with this young man of yours?" Harvey said. I had to admit he was game, but this was the opening my mother had been looking for.

"What indeed?" she said. "That is something you might give a little thought to, Harvey. I see your daughters are all nicely settled, your brother Paul is an inspector of local transport. Selwyn must be the only member of the family who hasn't yet enjoyed your generous help." Now that Harvey was on the run, she was almost happy. She smiled, she made small, graceful gestures with her hands. "There's nothing available for him in the Town Hall, is there?" she said. "He has a good brain,

he's industrious. What's more, he can keep his mouth shut."
She offered this with a curious nod of the head.

Its effect on Harvey was instant and terrible. He gaped, he
turned pale, and, grasping his briefcase firmly under his arm,
he shot off into the traffic. "I'll see what I can do," he wailed,
running.

"That's all right, then," my mother said.

"Is that why we came out this morning?" I said.

"You're getting sharper, Selwyn," my mother said. "We
might make something of you yet. Stand up straight."

That is how I came to work in the Clerk's Department of
the Town Hall. There all the legal work was handled, all the
local bylaws interpreted, all the niceties of government at this
level discussed. It was also the place where the aldermen and
councillors came for their supplies of stationery.

Small amounts of paper and ink were appropriate, I suppose, for the men of power to conduct their legal council affairs.
It was my responsibility to give them such supplies. I was
astonished by the appetites shown by these men. Week after
week they took away truckloads of paper, gallons of ink, relief
nibs by the many gross, erasers, wooden rulers, loose-leaf
binders, pencils, ruled foolscap and unruled foolscap, enve-
lopes of every size and color. It seemed I was in charge of an
Aladdin's cave of office supplies.

"Am I supposed to keep note of these withdrawals?" I asked
Henry Morgan, an old man who had worked in the office for
over thirty years.

"You are supposed to keep your eyes shut," he said.

I took for my own use a notebook of impressive thickness
with a hard blue cover. It gave every indication of weight and
permanence. As our leaders took away their paper troves, I
would enter, neatly and ostentatiously, a set of meaningless
ciphers against their names. After a while my colleagues noticed
this habit and grew restive. Some of them, having cultivated
powers of inattention and quietness over periods of long dura-
tion, were cautious of anything that might alter the smooth
groove of custom. Others were suspicious that I was so far
exceeding my duties that I might jump over their heads and
achieve promotion—something that had not happened in the

office for ten years. Wesley Graham was one of these. Wesley was a tall and personable young man who all day bustled about the Town Hall, his expression alert, his stride brisk. In his hand he carried a bundle of documents chosen at random from some file. His travels took him into every office in the building, and he was able to bring back to us innumerable items of news and interest. This was all he did.

"What are you writing in that notebook?" he asked me one day. He hovered like a hawk over the soft, expected prey of my answer.

"It's a wise man, Wesley," I said, "who knows his own father."

I do not know why I said this, except that I had no better reply in mind. It threw Wesley Graham into wild confusion. He gasped, he hissed, he puffed his cheeks, he clutched his documents with both hands to his chest. "You'd better be careful," he bleated. I thought he was going to cry, but he went to his desk and buried his head in his arms. My colleagues, disturbed by this small drama, went back with unusual seriousness to their newspapers.

"What did you mean by that—" Henry Morgan asked me some days later—"'It's a wise man who knows his own father?'"

"Nothing, Henry," I said. "I wouldn't like to say I meant anything profound or ominous."

He looked at me uncertainly. "I don't know," he said. "I don't know at all. You're a deep one."

It was later that week that my Uncle Harvey came in. I went to meet him. "Good morning, Councillor Lockwood," I said. "Let me take your coat."

It was raining heavily outside, and my Uncle Harvey stood in his own small pool. Rain dripped from his hat, his nose, the hem of his coat. "No, no," he said. "My business won't take long."

This surprised me, for he was fond of making statements about his acumen, his probity, and his general superiority when compared to other men. And when he wanted supplies from my cave he needed at least twice as much as other customers. I awaited his pleasure.

"How are you getting on here, Selwyn?" he asked. "Are you happy? I wouldn't like to think that I had put a young man of promise and ambition into a dead-end job like this." He laid a hand like a flatfish on my shoulder, and a wet smile struggled onto his face.

"I'm fine here," I said. "Very happy."

"No, no," he said. "I can see that you're out of place. A boy of your intellect and energy is lost here. I've had a word with the Town Clerk, and you'll be working with him from tomorrow, in his own office, where he can keep an eye on you and guide you."

"Thank you," I said.

My Uncle Harvey wrapped his wet coat about him and prepared to leave. "Selwyn," he said piteously, "get rid of that blue notebook. The other councillors might object to it. It could be misunderstood."

"Certainly, Uncle," I said. "It shall go at once."

So it was that I entered the Clerk's Office, the center of power, the heart of the web. The next morning I walked through the general office and those who had been my colleagues greeted me according to their temperaments.

"How did you do it?" said Henry Morgan, his expression composed equally of admiration and bewilderment. He sat at his desk, his copy of the *Guardian* folded so many times that only the crossword was visible. I would miss old Henry Morgan. On slack winter afternoons we had read together some of the novels of Thomas Hardy, and he had just introduced me to *The Turn of the Screw* and *The Aspern Papers*.

"Luck, Henry," I said, "and an inborn talent for the devious."

"You're a dark horse," he said. "You'll take some watching."

I flicked a wink at his amiable gaze, tapped the Clerk's door, and walked in.

Mr. Felton was sitting in his chair behind a scrupulously neat desk, leather-topped. He had before him a sheet of paper. Mr. Maynard Felton was short, trimly made, perhaps sixty years old. He could move quickly, with long, sharp strides. His suits were immaculate, his linen precise, his skin pink and clear. The most obvious thing about him was his baldness, or, more correctly, his elaborate coiffure. He let his silver hair grow very

6

long at the back and sides of his head and then brought it to the crown, the strands meeting in a crest that ran the length of his dome. Beneath the plastered strands of hair, his naked skull gleamed. It was at this carefully disguised tonsure I stared while awaiting his questions. They were very general. He was interested in my family, in my ambitions and my curiosity. At length he seemed satisfied.

"You'll sit at that desk over there," he said.

"Thank you, Mr. Felton," I said.

"Have you brought that blue notebook with you?" he said.

"What blue notebook?" I said.

We got on very well together. I can't say we were friends, but I studied him closely. He was, for example, easily disturbed. His wife gave him a new fountain pen and, since he was very clumsy in practical matters, it became my responsibility to fill it when necessary. Once, in a spirit of experiment, I used not ink but a glutinous adhesive that came to us in bottles. Mr. Felton could not write with the pen, shook it venomously, swore, turned red, damned all pens, and went home for the day. I learned that he was allergic to the smell of oranges, and on one occasion when I wished him gone for an hour or so I ostentatiously peeled an orange and sucked it noisily. Mr. Felton rose in nausea from his seat, clapped his starched white handkerchief to his face, shouted, "You dirty pig!" and rushed, retching, from the room. In these and other ways, I began to have some control over the affairs of the office. In particular, I observed his clothes, which were beautiful and orthodox. I began to feel in me the onset of dandyism.

One day Mr. Felton came to work wearing his brown tweed, a cream shirt with a paisley necktie, and the finest pair of brown shoes I had ever seen. I admired them.

"I bought them at my brother's shop," Mr. Felton said. Mr. Felton had two brothers—Bennion, who kept the shoe shop, and Elwyn, who was a butcher. All three had come to our town from Cardiganshire when they were young men, and had prospered.

"How much would a pair like that cost, Mr. Felton?" I said.

I didn't want to know. I was giving him a chance to boast a little, but the idiot overplayed it. He laughed. His laugh implied that I had ambitions to purchase such shoes and that these ambitions were ridiculous. His laughter was brief and dismissive. "You can't afford shoes like this, boy," he said.

At lunchtime, I told my mother of this remark. Since I had joined the ranks of the comparatively wealthy, she had been notably more congenial, had sometimes even asked my opinion on unimportant matters. Her eyes gleamed. She was the most competitive woman I have ever known; in her was the spirit of a great and cruel general. "So that's what he thinks," she said. "Put clean socks on. I'll see you outside the Town Hall at five o'clock."

"We don't finish until five-thirty," I said.

"Five o'clock," she said. My mother was convinced that there was no man-made law she could not countermand merely by ignoring it.

First we went to John Montague's, a tailor shop whose doors were sumptuous and hushed—they closed behind us with the sound of paper money. There we bought a suit of such elegance that when I tried it on I could not find myself in the mirror. Of Irish thornproof, it was a closely woven heather mixture, subtle and distinguished. I was astonished to find that my wrists did not protrude several inches below the sleeves. We bought a shirt and a tie of equal splendor. My mother engaged to pay for these luxuries over a period of twelve months.

"Now," she said, "for Bennion Felton."

Bennion Felton did not look like his brother. He was round and comfortable, and years of bending at other people's feet had given him a stoop. He sent toward us one of his assistants, Alfie Edwards, a thin boy I had once to beat up for cheating at marbles. When we were small, of course.

My mother sent him reeling with an iron glance. "I'll see Mr. Felton," she said.

Bennion Felton came forward, recognizing a customer of unusual mettle.

"I'll see some of your very best brown shoes," my mother said. "For my son."

"For this young man?" said Bennion. "Our best shoes are rather expensive, Madam."

"We'll see them," said my mother. Queen Victoria could have taken lessons from her when it came to dealing with lesser mortals.

"He has a very large foot," said Bennion persuasively. We remained silent. He shrugged his shoulders. Soon the floor was littered with shoes. None of them looked like Mr. Felton's admired footwear.

"I think we might like to try a pair like those you sold your brother recently," my mother said. "Rather a decent brogue."

Bennion Felton brought them. They were beyond footwear—they were the shoes of gods. He named a price so far in excess of my monthly salary that inside I turned pale, though I did my best to look as if I bought such things by the dozen pairs.

My mother did not show any trepidation, whatsoever. "We'll take them," she said, "since it seems unlikely there will be better in this shop."

Crushed, little Bennion wrapped the shoes, took the moncy, bowed us out of his shop.

"I've been saving up," my mother said as we walked home. "It doesn't look as if you're going to grow anymore, so you might as well wear something decent."

My grandmother examined my finery, approved the quality, hoped that its purchase would coincide with a new, more graceful physical control on my part. Excessive size she felt to be a moral flaw and I must do my best to atone for it.

The next morning, dressed in my new finery, I breakfasted early and walked down to Anton's. Anton's was where men of fashion in our town had their hair cut. Until that day my grandmother had cut my hair. Anton's was empty.

"Good morning—uh, sir," said Anton, puzzled. It was the garb and the assurance it brought me that puzzled Anton.

"Good morning, Bertie," I said to Anton.

I had known Anton since we were six years old. Most of that time he'd been Bertie Turner.

"I thought it was you," he said. "You look really good. You really do."

"See what you can do with the old top end, Bert," I said. "Something conservative and high-class—what you might call a classic cut. Nothing foppish."

He cut beautifully. My entry into the office that morning was sensational. Men reeled away. Wesley Graham turned ashen and sobbed openly.

Mr. Felton was properly appreciative. He looked me up and down, he walked around me. I was suitably modest, merely lifting an interrogatory eyebrow.

"There's a committee meeting this afternoon," he said. "You'd better come, look after my papers, take a few notes, that sort of thing. You'll soon pick it up."

After the meeting, Henry Morgan stopped me outside the Clerk's Office. He told me he was worried about my welfare. "You meet a funny class of person at those gatherings," he said.

"What do you mean?" I said.

"All they think of is money," he said. "That's all Felton ever thought of."

I told him I could handle the idea of money, but he was not consoled. "You might think that uncle of yours—Harvey Lockwood—is a cunning one with silver," he said. "Let me tell you, Harvey Lockwood is a pygmy compared to old Felton—a feather, a hammer of air, a financial cripple, an infant mewling in the dark, an idiot counting pennies. I could go on."

I invited him to continue.

"Who," he said, "built the Old People's Homes?"

"Patrick Parry & Sons, Ltd.," I said.

"Right," said Henry. "And who built the two new schools down in the valley, and the hospital extension, and the bus shelter? Who has the contract for the new Civic Center, worth millions?"

"None other than that same Patrick Parry," I said.

"Maynard Felton and Patrick Parry are as thick as thieves," Henry said. "Until Maynard became Town Clerk, Parry was just an ordinary carpenter. Work it out for yourself. You know what happens to men who worship money."

I did. They grew rich. The next day I bought shares in Patrick Parry & Sons, Ltd.—my first investment.

"He won't take it with him," Henry said on a later day, when we were again discussing Mr. Felton's money. "He won't even be able to keep it in this town. It will all go back to Cardigan."

"Why Cardigan?" I asked.

"He married a girl from Cardigan," Henry Morgan said. "After his first wife died. She came up to keep house for him—years younger than he is. A distant cousin. Oh, they're clannish in Cardigan—they're close. They wanted someone right up next to him to keep an eye on his bank balance; they won't let any of that out of the family. It will go back to Cardigan. He has no children, you see."

"You mean it was a plot?" I said. "They meant him to marry this girl?"

"Of course," Henry Morgan said. "Imagine the farms they can buy with Felton's money. They certainly didn't want him to marry anyone else, some stranger who'd keep all that lovely clover for herself. What a clan! Mind, she looks after him, I'll say that. She's a good wife, the girl from Cardigan."

That winter was long and stern. I remember it with some affection, because, walking to the office one morning, I slipped on a treacherous patch of ice beneath the snow and twisted my knee. I had to walk with the help of a stick, and when I recovered I kept the stick. It became recognizable, helped to define me. I still have it, although more expensive models have long since replaced it in the shops. Mr. Felton caught influenza, struggled on, wheezing and coughing, and then took to his bed. At the end of the week, on Friday morning, I collected those papers that demanded his attention and took them up to Mr. Felton's house.

"Watch out," Henry Morgan said as I passed through the outer office, buttoning with care my new British warm, adjusting my scarf. "Look out for that girl from Cardigan."

Mr. Felton's was a large, detached house, built of dressed blocks of the local gray stone. Quiet, rich, impressive. I rang the bell, and the girl from Cardigan answered. She was hardly a girl, but she was much younger than Mr. Felton. She was dark, slender, rather severe. She let me in, and I went upstairs to Mr. Felton's bedroom. He was in bed, his features sharper than usual and his skin the color of rice. The furniture was heavy, gleaming. Mr. Felton wore on his head a conical nightcap. I had seen such in illustrated copies of Dickens. We began to go through the papers.

"These," I said, "are all straightforward and require only your signature."

He looked them through very carefully and signed them.

"These," I said, "require some decision from you. As far as possible, I've brought necessary supporting documents."

He told me what his decisions were.

"This smaller group," I said, "is outside my understanding and is obviously for your consideration."

He read them through with the greatest care, word by word. I had read them equally carefully.

"Are you sure, boy," he said, "that you don't understand these?"

I gave him a blank and blue-eyed stare. "Certain," I said.

Mr. Felton got steadily worse. Each week I took him his papers. Mrs. Felton would bring coffee to me, and chocolate biscuits. He would work his way laboriously through those documents that were concerned with his work at the office and then spend a very long time over the papers that detailed his more profitable activities.

One Friday he leaned back on his pillows and watched me sip my coffee. Mrs. Felton had just brought it and had vanished silently down the wide stairs.

"My wife is much younger than I," he said. "My first wife died."

"So I understand," I said.

"She's my cousin's daughter," he said, "come up from the country to look after me."

"Is that so?" I said.

"It isn't decent for a man and woman to live in the same house unmarried," he said. "I could see that."

"Why not," I said, "and you related to her."

He gave me a quick glance. "There's more to it," he said. "You're a sharp boy and a big boy, but there's more to it."

I thought he was going to tell me all about his money, but he didn't say another word. Mrs. Felton let me out; the heavy door didn't make a sound behind me.

Maynard Felton's bronchitis turned into pneumonia and he died, just after Christmas. Henry Morgan and I, representing the office staff, went to his funeral.

"Did you see the two Felton brothers?" said Henry as we went back to the office. "Looked pretty blue, and it wasn't just the cold. They were thinking of all that lovely money that they won't get." Henry sounded very happy. We walked through the freezing dark, and he hummed and whistled all the way.

Mr. Felton's house was sold. The girl from Cardigan returned demurely to that green county, her luggage full of money. Sometimes I've felt I can see the road to Cardigan, green as banknotes, shining under the moon. Patrick Parry & Sons went bankrupt, but I'd sold my shares by then.

That was my early education in politics—sound, practical, informative. I've done well, I admit it. But I wouldn't say I am a self-made man. No, no, I was well taught. I was very well taught.

A Flight
of Geese

My Uncle Wynford wasn't
really my uncle; he was my great-uncle, my grandmother's
brother. I used to visit him often on my way home from school.
He lived in a small house at the edge of the village with his
wife and two daughters. He also had two sons, but they lived
in London and one of them was a famous footballer, an International. A color photograph of him, wearing his International
cap and shirt, his arms folded across his chest, stood on the
sideboard. My uncle had given up regular work when he was
a young man. He had come home unexpectedly early from the
engine room at the steelworks and announced his philosophy
of leisure. "Anne," he had said to his wife, "I shall not be going
to work again. There's too much talk about the dignity of labor.
One life is all we have and I'm not spending mine in senseless
toil." And he never did.

Not that he was an idle man. His garden was neat and
orderly; his workbench, in the shed at the end of the garden,
was swept free of dust and shavings; his tools, worn and
polished with use, all had their proper place, and were sharp
and clean. He could build a freestone wall, clear a chimney,
repair plumbing. He was marvellously inventive with metal and
stone, those old elements. But most of all he liked to work with
wood. His hands held wood intimately, as if he knew all of
its lost warmth and offered with his fingers and the flat of his

15

palm a consolation for the tragic falling of trees. He made six crimson soup spoons for my grandmother, carved from the one piece of yew, polished hard and smooth. And he made her a little footstool for her use in chapel on Sundays. Many Sunday evenings I sat on that little stool, my head well below the top of the pew, noiselessly sucking a mint, reading a comic book while interminable sermons thundered above me.

Uncle Wynford made a stool for himself, too—a larger one. His was secular, not intended for Sunday use. It was painted in the most brilliant and glittering colors. The panel of the seat was decorated with an oval centerpiece, a landscape in which a lake of raucous blue lay beneath impossibly dramatic mountains. Water lilies grew close at hand, and birds—swallows, probably—performed their frozen arabesques above the water. Far away the little, leaning sails of yachts and skiffs stood white against the hills. Complex patterns, like those in the *Book of Kells,* covered the legs and the undersurface. My uncle normally carried this stool about with him. A short man, he found it useful to stand on in crowds, but mostly he just sat on it whenever he stopped to talk.

For his finest art was conversation. He loved above all else to be among a small circle of old friends, who made together a pattern of articulate life, each in his turn leading the discussion or telling a story, the others an essential, encouraging chorus. At all aspects of this activity my uncle was a master. Nobody could listen more intently to tales told many times before, nobody could time an urgent question more subtly, nobody else could invent such marvellous, rich detail. His voice was like an instrument. He could use it to entice, to chill, to bombard. On early autumn mornings he sat among his friends down at the square, he on his wooden throne, they squatting or sprawled at length on the warm stone.

It was my habit then to go to school very early. I used to run almost all the way, using an exaggerated stride and a very upright stance, arms bent high at the elbow, trying to look like Paavo Nurmi in a photograph I had seen in an old book about the Olympic Games. I was running across the square one morning, driving off the toes just like Nurmi, when my Uncle

16

Wynford called me. "Don't run, boy," he said. "You've no need to run. You have plenty of time."

I tried to tell him that I liked getting to school early, that I liked being alone on the playground when it was silent and empty and the windows of the school were without life, but he just shook his head and held my hand, so that I had to stand by him. I wore a white shirt and gray trousers, and my shadow was very long and thin in the sun.

After a while Mr. Carrington spoke. He was Frankie Carrington's grandfather. He had been a butcher, and kept snuff in a little silver box. He had a walking stick with a handle made of antler and was in every way precise and gentlemanly.

"Going up the street last evening," he said, "I saw Arthur Baker standing at his door with his dog—you know, that blue-roan cocker. It was sitting at Arthur's feet, near the front door. I hadn't seen the dog for some time." Mr Carrington smiled as he looked back in his mind and saw himself talking to Arthur Baker. " 'Well, Arthur,' I said, 'I haven't seen that dog of yours for some time, but there she is, safe and sound.' "

"Quick-tempered fellow," said Ginty Willis. "Arthur Baker has a very quick temper. All the Bakers have. Like living in a box of matches in their house."

"What did he say?" asked my Uncle Wynford. "What did Arthur say to you?"

"That's just it," said Mr. Carrington, leaning forward, widening his eyes, tapping himself on the knee to impress us. "He said nothing at first. He rushed down the path, and then, I swear, he almost shouted at me."

"Angry, was he?" said Ginty Willis. "Oh, a terrible quick temper."

"Not so much angry as puzzled," Mr. Carrington said. "And, yes, a bit frightened."

"Frightened?" my uncle said. "Why should he have been frightened?"

"Because the dog wasn't there!" Mr. Carrington said. "What do you think of that? Not there! 'What are you saying?' Arthur Baker shouted. 'My dog was killed a fortnight ago. Run over by a truck. What do you mean there she is, safe and sound?' And boys, when I looked again, there was no dog anywhere.

17

Gave me quite a turn." Mr. Carrington pursed his lips and took out his snuffbox.

"Was it dark?" said Selby Davis belligerently. He wasn't really bullying; sometimes he stammered, so he pushed his words out quickly and roughly before he tripped over them.

Mr. Carrington considered. "Not dark," he said, "but certainly more than dusk. The house—the Bakers' house—was in deep shadow."

"Could have been a shadow you saw," said Selby Davis.

"It could have been," agreed Mr. Carrington, "but it looked very much like Arthur Baker's dog."

"Arthur was very fond of that dog," said my uncle, "and the dog adored him. There was a great bond between them. It could have been some form of manifestation you saw, Jimmy." I hadn't known Mr. Carrington's name was Jimmy, so I looked at him carefully, to see if it suited him.

Eddie D'Arcy progressed across the square, more a parade than a walk. His dark suit was superbly cut, his white shirt was dazzling, his silk tie was rich and sombre, his expensive black shoes utterly without flaw or spot. Despite the perfection of the morning, he carried an umbrella, rolled tight as a sword.

"Good morning, gentlemen," said Eddie, his vowels without fault, his dignity unassailable.

"Good morning, Eddie," the men said, smiling and nodding.

Eddie moved, full-sailed, out of sight, toward the office where he worked as a lawyer.

"Clever chap, Eddie," said my uncle. He turned again to Mr. Carrington. "Jimmy," he said, "I'm prepared to believe that what you saw up at the Bakers was a manifestation. Stands to reason that an animal's identity is bound up with its sense of place, and, in the case of a domestic animal like a dog, with its owner." He warmed to his topic. "Our lives—the lives of human beings—are astonishingly manipulated by animals. It is useless to ignore the fact that our lives are deeply influenced by those of animals. Take Eddie D'Arcy as an example."

"What about Eddie D'Arcy?" asked Ginty Willis.

"Did I ever tell you about the D'Arcys' goose?" my uncle said.

Nobody answered.

"Old Mrs. D'Arcy bought a gosling to fatten for Christmas," said Uncle Wynford. "Eddie was a little boy then. The bird had the run of the field at the back of the house. It grew and prospered—oh, it grew into a magnificent goose." We could see that my uncle still admired the bird's every feather. "Yes," he said, "it was a splendid bird."

"I've done it myself, often," said Selby Davis, in his angry voice. "I prefer goose to any other bird. Properly cooked, a goose is lovely."

"This was an unusual goose," my uncle said. "Called at the back door every morning for its food, answered to its name. An intelligent creature. Eddie's sisters tied a blue silk ribbon around its neck and made a pet of it. It displayed more personality and understanding than you'd believe possible in a bird. Came Christmas, of course, and they couldn't kill it."

"Couldn't kill it?" Mr. Carrington said, his professional sense outraged. "It's not all that difficult. The best way. . . ."

My uncle stopped him with a wave of his hand, as if conducting music. "They knew how to kill it," he said, "but they were unable to do so. On moral grounds, if you like. They were fond of it. They loved it. The goose lived another twenty years; Eddie grew up with it. They all cried when, at last, it died. Except Eddie, of course."

"Why not Eddie?" someone asked.

"You know how particular Eddie is?" Uncle Wynford said. "Such clothes, such a dandy? How not a mote of dust shall settle on his linen, how his handkerchief must be pressed to a mathematical nicety? Imagine how it must have been for him, living in that house with an elderly, dictatorial goose. You ever tried to house-train a goose, Ginty?"

"I have not," said Ginty. "I imagine it can't be done."

"It can't," said my uncle, laughing.

"Geese are pretty bright," I said. "They're good guards. Some geese saved Rome from the invaders."

"The boy's right," said Mr. Carrington. "Well done, boy. I can see you're going to be a great scholar."

"I had a cousin in Cardiganshire who was an expert with geese," my uncle said after a silence. "Kept all the varieties in his time. People used to come from all over the country to buy breeding stock from him. Oh, what a sight to see his flocks on the moors—great flocks of geese, marching like Prussians! He used to clip their wings at the elbow so they couldn't fly, and then, once they were old enough, out they'd go on the open moors, white geese, gray geese. They never strayed. At dusk they'd come high-stepping into his yard and the whole mountain would be full of their voices. I often stayed with him when I was young.

"He sent us a goose every year—two geese: one for Michaelmas and another for Christmas, always trussed and ready for cooking. He used to send them by bus—a bewildering journey, with many changes—but none of them ever failed to reach us. I used to wait here, on the square, for the bus to come in from Brecon toward late afternoon. The conductor would hand me a large hamper with our goose inside, and I'd stagger home with it. We used to cook it on a spit, rotating it in front of a blaze of a fire, a pan beneath to catch the melting fat. We took turns at basting as it spun slowly—first one way, then the other—so that it wouldn't burn. Every Michaelmas and every Christmas for years. What feasts we had then! Nor was that the end of the goose's usefulness. After the cooking we put the solidified goose grease in jars and kept it as a cure for sore throats and chest colds and bronchitis. I can remember my mother rubbing it on my bare chest and throat when I was a small boy. I can remember its gross smell, the thick feel of the grease on my skin. I hated that, although the old people swore by it as a curative.

"And even the bed I slept on owed its comfort to my cousin's geese, for the bed was stuffed with feathers from his birds. My mother made a huge envelop of blue-and-white striped ticking and filled it with goose feathers, making the whole thing plump and soft as a cloud. We all sleep well when we're young, but nobody could have slept softer and deeper than I did in my goose-feather bed."

My uncle held out his hand in front of him. "You see this hand?" he asked. "The hand is a superb instrument. This hand of mine can do all manner of things: it can wield a hammer, pick up a pin, it can point a chisel to the exact splitting place of a stone, it can create, it can destroy. My cousin's hands were to do with geese. He had huge hands. Here, on the inside of his thumb and forefinger, he had long calluses, incredibly hard, from feathering geese. Every week he would kill and pluck some of his birds for market, and many more near Christmas and other busy times. He had slaughtered thousands over the years. And when he plucked them he did it swiftly, expertly, and the soft flesh would not be bruised or torn when he finished. I've seen him kill and dress hundreds of birds. He was an artist."

"How old was he, Wynford?" Mr. Carrington asked.

"Not a lot older than I," said my uncle. "Seven or eight years. But that's a lot when you're young. He was already at work on the farm when I was a young boy visiting there."

"What's he doing now?" asked Selby Davis.

"He's dead," my uncle said softly. "Yes, he's dead these many years." He shifted on his painted stool. He was far away, visiting an old sadness. "He's been dead for years," he repeated. "One Christmas he had many geese, and he set to work early, day after day, killing and preparing them. The weather was intolerably cold. The mountains had a fall of snow, two feet deep and deeper in drifts. It never stopped freezing. Night and day not a gust of wind—only the deep stillness of frost. My cousin kept the dead birds in a long barn, where they hung in rows, heads down. The bitter cold worried my cousin. It was bringing in the wild things off the hills, the rats and foxes. He found himself staying more and more near his filling barn.

"One night he awoke from sleep, bright awake at once, certain that something was wrong. It was just after three in the morning. He hurried into his thick clothes and wrapped a blanket over his shoulders. There wasn't a sound in the yard; even the living birds were silent. The brilliant snow threw back every gleam of light, redoubled it, so the night was unnaturally lit. The barn door was locked and safe. Nothing was out of place. He opened the door and went in. The dead geese hung in their rows before him, untouched, pallid. The night was pitilessly still. My cousin moved along the stiff files, alert, waiting for something to happen.

"Then, in the cold barn, as if from high above him, he heard the call of geese, far away, the crying of wild geese out of the empty sky. He could hear them clearly, although he knew they were not there. He did not move. In an instant the barn was full of their loud honking; their flailing wings beat under the sturdy roof. He closed his eyes in terror, he wrapped his arms about his bent head, and through his barn flew the heavy skeins of great, invisible birds. Their crying filled his ears; the still air was buffeted by their plunging flight, on and on, until the last bodiless goose was flown and the long, wild voices were gone. He stood in the cold of his barn and opened his eyes. What he saw was this: he saw the hanging corpses of his own geese, every one swaying, every one swinging gently. And that was the most frightening of all.''

My uncle sighed. ''Poor old boy,'' he said. ''Poor old lad. After a while they took him to Swansea, to the mental hospital, and he died there.''

''How do you know this?'' asked Ginty Willis.

''He told me,'' said Uncle Wynford. ''I went down to see him, and he told me. He was a young man, only thirty-two when he died. He had killed thousands of geese, thousands of them.''

''What was his name, Uncle?'' I asked. I stood in the warm day as cold as if I were in the heart of that long-dead winter and were standing under the roof among the swaying corpses of Christmas geese.

''Good God!'' my uncle said. ''Are you still here? Get to school, get to school! You'll be late.'' I turned and ran.

All day my friends were indolent in the heat of the quiet classroom, moving sleepily through their work, but all I could see were the high arrows of the streaming geese, all I could hear was their faint and melancholy crying, and the imagined winter was all about me.

Sing It Again,
Wordsworth

Last night I awoke with a troubled mind. It seemed to me that I had no roots, that there was no place, however distant, to which I could turn at so desolate a moment. Despite its familiarity, the years I've had of touching and using its furniture, its known sounds, I awoke lost in my own room. The house seemed to hang alone in space. I got out of bed and walked to the window, heavily, groaning a little, my feet turned out like those of an old man. The moon was high. There was light enough to show deep shadows under the bushes and to make sharp the angles of walls, but I recognized nothing. The world stopped at the boundaries of the garden. To imagine the solid lane which passes my gate, its hedges of elder and hawthorn, its green ditch, was an impossible act of the will. I tried in an agony of memory to recall the faces of the men who would soon be cycling in the dawn light along the lane to work. I could not remember one of them, though they are men I've known for years.

This house was built for me twenty years ago. I made its garden from the untouched meadow; the shrubs and trees grow where I planted them. I marked the new course of the little stream at the boundary, dug it out by hand, plank by plank bridged it. It is my home. Yet I went back to bed unable to imagine the feel of the spade in my hand, unable to think of the color of the roses already abundant in the borders. I turned on my side knowing I would not sleep again.

23

The weathers and scenes of childhood remain long in a man's mind, and I tried to remember them; but when I searched among the images of the past I found myself too far away. I have travelled away from those places for half a lifetime. Their summers are thin and cold, their voices inaudible. It was then that I realized there is no place mine without the asking for it, no place where I belong by clear right.

Sitting in the late afternoon sun, lounging, relaxed, I can smile at that fear in the night. I know that if I had to choose at this moment a place to be native to, I would be unable to decide. I think of the Dysynni Valley, the loveliest in Wales. I see the Dysynni River winding inland from its salt lagoon through the soft, coastal flats above Tywyn, past the village of Llanegryn where the squat little church, a holy place for over a thousand years, lies under a buffeting wind. Then the river cuts directly into the heart of Cader Idris, the high, wild moorland. Round-shouldered cormorants fly in from the sea until they reach Bird Rock and they sit there, on the harsh cliff above the river, alert for migratory sea trout. I would travel farther, the austerity of the mountains each side of me; I would climb to Castell-y-Bere, aloof on its long rock, its great walls fallen. When I was sixteen I stood one night near this castle, on the lip of a stone ridge high above the Dysynni, and I saw another river, one invisible by day, run straight and flat over the meadows and into the eye of the moon. I could not believe what I saw. I climbed down the steep face, leaped the fence, ran into the visionary water. It was quite dry. I ran in the brittle stubble and dusty grass of a harvested field. What I had thought a river was the light of the moon reflected in the webs of millions of ground-covering spiders, each filament luminous with borrowed moonlight. I stood in the middle of the glittering track and looked the moon in the face.

Or I could be a man of Dorset, that secretive, beautiful county. We used to live there, near Sherborne. We rented a cottage in a lane between Yetminister and Thornford. In a place of beautiful stone houses ours was ugly.

It was over a hundred years old but time had done nothing to soften the raw brick of its walls. It had been a laborer's cottage, built for a man who would spend all daylight in the fields. It was not meant to be attractive; it was meant for poverty. Its rooms were mean and damp, its windows narrow, fires burned reluctantly in its niggardly grates. In summer a climbing rose, the good old noisette Gloire de Dijon, ramped over the south wall and reached the roof, filling the air with nostalgic perfume. Its buff flowers lasted through June and occasional faded blooms hung on bravely into September. It was as old as the cottage and its only decorative element. We had no neighbors, but old Mr. Ayling, who farmed nearby, sometimes spoke to us. He let us walk in his pastures, showed us where the horse mushrooms grew, enormous, flat, creamy, over an inch thick. We'd put one in the pan and fry it as if it were a steak.

One Saturday I walked away from the house, past Beer Hackett church and up Knighton Hill. The year had begun to turn into spring and fat buds were waiting on the trees. A cold sun shone, windflowers were growing, frail and white, in sheltered places. I marched through Lillington and up into hilly country near Bishop's Caundle. Leaning on a field gate I looked down into the valley, imagining it turned greener as I watched. Then, from the narrow head of the top field, the hounds ran. Sixteen couple streaming in freedom together, the full, beautiful pack, certain of their line, unstoppable in their galloping. Behind them, riding hard, came the boldest members of the hunt. I could see old Mr. Ayling. He had lost his hat and his long white hair was shining in the sun. Too far away to hear the sounds of the chase, I watched their brilliant, silent charge through the valley. It was exhilarating, heartwarming. I stood on a bar of the gate and almost cheered.

A movement among the fists of the new green ferns close by distracted me. It was a small dog fox, hardly more than a cub. I could see his wedge-shaped head. He came out of the hedge, grinning, measuring me with a quizzical little eye, and sat down, settling himself carefully on his thin hams. Vaguely embarrassed, I stepped off the gate and stood near him. He didn't move. Together we watched the disappearing hunt, together we watched the stragglers vanish awkwardly into the bottom wood. The little fox was panting lightly, but he was not distressed. He got up, gave me a sardonic glance, and trotted jauntily down the lane, his brush swinging. It was a revelation to me. I saw that I was on the side of the fox. Such experiences make a man native to a place; I could live in Dorset.

Or in Seattle, I could live there. To think of that Pacific city, ringed by conical hills and filled with the sounds of water, makes me homesick. I liked Seattle from the day I flew in. When I'd been there about a week I went into a tackle shop to buy a fishing license.

"Are you an alien?" asked the sad, middle-aged lady as she opened her book of licenses.

I was astonished and then ashamed. I had to admit I was an alien.

"It's more when you're an alien," she said. "That will be seven dollars seventy-five."

I gave her the money.

"Don't be sore," she said."I've been an alien fifty years. Ever since my parents brought me over from Huddersfield."

I got in the Volkswagen and drove out to Quillayute, a little place on the Olympic Peninsula, and the next morning I took three jack salmon out of the Bogachiel before breakfast. The sun was not up, and I stood on a rock in midstream and threw my spinner into the margin of a fast current and the fish came to me. I went all over Washington State and I took steelhead from the Skagit River and the Stillaguamish River and cutthroat from Chopaka Lake and Jameson Lake and the Hood Canal. And later, sailing out of Aberdeen, I took big salmon from the ocean, but I was still an alien. Oh, I could live out there, just as I could live at Summer Cove, County Cork, a mile from Kinsale, on the north shore of Kinsale Harbor.

I'm deceiving myself, I know that. The little Dorset fox and the lady in the tackle shop were right; I'm an outsider and an alien. I have this insatiable thirst for other places. I cannot remain at peace for long in one place. I've known this for some time, I see it plain. I work alone, traveling haphazardly the length of the country, shake hands with people I'll never see again, come home. Sometimes I travel by train or plane, but mostly I drive.

Next week I shall drive to Birmingham, knowing every yard of the way. Once I'd have got out my maps and guides, plotted the journey with care, set off early so that I could see every ancient landmark, fine church, old house on the way. For a happy morning I'd have balanced the attractions of one route against those of another. But that's all done now. Next week I'll drive to Birmingham taking the fast roads and the journey will take just over two hours. I shan't stop anywhere.

I went to college in Birmingham. I knew the place well when I was young.

My homeward journeys, often late at night, are nearly always unplanned and instinctive. Last year I was working on the North Wales coast, near Prestatyn. I finished in the early evening and decided not to stay for dinner. I paid my hotel bill and carried my bags to the car. I wiped the midges from the windscreen, sat in the car, fastened the safety belt, and went. I was going to make a fast run. It had been raining earlier, but the evening was brilliantly dry and sharp, the air washed clear. A few clouds moved out at sea, low on the skyline. I sat upright and relaxed, utterly at peace, knowing the extremities of the car as I knew my own skin, driving with the fingertips. I came down the Ruthin road, the A-525, neatly and circumspectly, with an amused caution, knowing I could put the car wherever I liked, sensitive even to the grain of the road.

At Ruthin I turned off for Corwen and Llangollen. It was dusk, and a cold, erratic wind began to get up. Soon, before I reached Oswestry, I switched on the headlights. The road was empty. I went straight down the marches through Welshpool and Newtown before hitting the A-44 at Crossgates. It was raining hard when I got to Kington. I stopped there and found a little coffeehouse still open, spoke a while with the sleepy young Italian waiter, and drifted gently out of town, the roads dark and wet. It was past midnight when I drove through Hereford. The heavy rain stopped as I was leaving the city. A policeman came out of the shop doorway, took off his wet coat, and shook it.

I knew where I was in general terms, but the darkness and the rain were making things difficult to recognize. I wanted to head for Gloucester through Peterstow and Ross-on-Wye, a road I've driven many times, but when I ran on to a long stretch of dual carriageway I knew I was lost. I wasn't worried.

I knew I'd meet familiar roads soon enough. I pushed hard down the wide road, the car dipping gently as it met small pools of water at the edge of the drying surfaces. Two coaches passed, travelling in the opposite direction, their interior lights bright. I saw people asleep in their seats, their heads lolling against windows. The dual carriageway ended and with it the sodium lights overhead. I began to swing down the bends of a narrower road, the weight of sudden darkness oppressive. It was raining again. The car rocked like a boat through the washing gutters and I hunched my shoulders against the hills I felt were steep and close on either side. One or two houses, unlit and blank, stood at the sides of the road. Then I saw the river. I'm a sucker for rivers. I stopped the car and got out. Wind lashed the ends of my coat, the rain stung in its gusts. It was a lovely river; swollen by storm, ominous, full to the lips of its grass banks, its loud, black thunder rolled in the channels of my ears.

I got the big torch out of the car and walked down the road. The one street of a village slept under the whipped rain and I walked right through, to the far end. Then, on the left hand, a marvelous abbey pushed its ruined walls into the darkness, very Gothic, very romantic. I let the straight beam of the torch climb on its stones and arches. I knew where I was. I was in Tintern, on the banks of the Wye, looking at Tintern Abbey. A miracle of the night had brought me there. A single light came from a distant hill farm, hanging in the darkness a long way up. I watched it for a long time, wondering what emergency had called its people awake at two in the morning. It went out and I was left alone, listening to the loud river and the swift noise of the rain. I danced a little soft-shoe shuffle at the side of the road, in honor of William Wordsworth.

Laughing, I ran back to the car, took off my soaked coat, and drove down to Chepstow. Soon I was sidling cautiously on to the M-4, heavy at that hour with groaning trucks out of Newport and Cardiff, and two hours later I was in bed.

Next week I shall drive straight up to Birmingham and straight back, unless I visit Arthur Marshalsea.

When I first went to college in Birmingham I lived in one of the hostels and Arthur Marshalsea had the room next to mine. His parents lived out at Sutton Coldfield, only a few miles away.

Arthur could have traveled each day, but he wanted to live
in college. He came into my room the first morning of term;
I was making my bed. He wanted to borrow a book, a dictionary. I could see that was an excuse. Arthur stood just inside
the door, dressed in a dark track suit with red flashes. He was
not tall, but very powerfully made, long-armed, deep-chested.
He spoke slowly, using a deep, cultured voice. It wasn't the
way he normally spoke, I could tell that. He was trying out
one of the many personalities a young man adopts before he
accepts the mask that best fits him, or, if he's lucky, presents
his own face to the world. He didn't open the dictionary I gave
him.

"Coming over to the dining hall?" he asked.

We walked over together and after that we did most things
together. Arthur had more pure energy than any other person
I've known. Most mornings I'd be the first to get up in our
building. I'd potter about for half an hour, relishing the slow
quiet of the early day, sit in my armchair and read, make a pot
of tea for myself and perhaps for Billy Notley, who came from
Worcester and took the same courses I did. I'd shave slowly,
feeling the pleasure of a long day stretching out in front of me.
I liked that morning silence, I liked my footsteps to echo
through the empty halls and corridors.

But when Arthur got up it was like an electric storm. At
once the place vibrated. Arthur would be singing, laughing out
of his window at friends on their way to breakfast; he would
be washing and shaving, surrounded by lather and steam, his
towels spinning and flapping; he would be out and off at a run,
springing over the ground. He ran everywhere. His knowledge
of the city and the countryside around was immense. Most free
afternoons we'd get out and Arthur would show me some
strange area, streets of small factories, full of old men skilled
in dying crafts; a long stretch of black canal, still, very quiet,
only a few yards from the city center; old markets where you
could buy cheeses, lengths of cloth, brass candlesticks black
with grime and age. I learned a lot about the city from Arthur.
In return I talked to him about plays and novels, went to the
theater with him, wrote most of his essays. We played for the
college soccer team, Arthur and I, he our one player of true

quality and I a competent midfield player. We played other teams around the Midlands, sometimes on Saturdays, often on Thursday afternoons.

One Saturday morning we played at Dudley, a Black Country town near Wolverhampton. It was in early March, and a week of rain had made the ground heavy and difficult, but that day I was possessed by something like inspiration. I ran as if fatigue were a myth, I passed and tackled with a perfect stylish accuracy, I went around opponents as if they were insubstantial as mist. I scored two goals in the first twenty minutes, one with a precise lob from a long way out. It seemed to me that I knew every bounce of the ball. Near the end of the game Arthur took the ball in our opponents' half, turned inside the fullback, and ran, huge leaping strides carrying him over the mud. I ran inside him, a couple of yards behind. Reaching the penalty area, he checked the ball and pushed it delicately into my path. It was a perfect pass, perfect in weight and speed. I hit the ball with a full swing of the right foot and I saw, as I fell, how it flew into the top corner of the net. It was there, a complete goal, before the goalkeeper had begun to make his leap. I can still recapture every moment of that thirty-year-old game. Afterward I took a bus into the city center and Arthur came with me.

The municipal art gallery was showing a visiting exhibition of paintings by Van Gogh. For the first time, all the great oils had been brought together, and suddenly I knew I wanted to see them, it was essential for me to see them. We climbed the steps and went in. I could see all the famous paintings I'd known only in reproductions and the sight of those intense and passionate statements set me eloquent. Moving from canvas to canvas I told Arthur of the splendor and individuality of Van Gogh's vision, of the unity of his composition, of the values he gave to the sun in this picture and that, of a thousand things I'd never thought of before but which were suddenly both simple and novel. It seemed to me then that I knew the purpose behind every stroke of the man's brush. In a few minutes I had collected a small, respectful audience. This didn't deter me. Aware of the farcical nature of the situation, I explored even wilder flights of invention and rhetoric, but while I was amused I thought that what I said was right and necessary, that there was little about art and life and Van Gogh which was unknown to me at that moment. It was an hour of serious and absurd play-acting. At the end I was exhausted. Arthur stepped up to me and shook my hand warmly.

"Young man," he said, "that was a privilege and a pleasure. You have given us all a rare insight into the workings of a creative mind. I hope you will not be offended if I give you this as a sign of my appreciation." He gave me a coin. I started to laugh, but Arthur held up his hand firmly, smiled at me as if he were some polite and well-intentioned stranger, and walked away. My other listeners pressed forward, murmured their gratitude, pushed their offerings into my hand. I held a solid fistful of currency here. When I got outside Arthur was waiting for me, leaning over the balustrade, laughing. We had enough money to visit the cinema and eat a generous dinner at a restaurant normally well out of our reach. Content and leisurely aristocrats, patrons and lovers of the arts, we arrived back late that night at our hostel.

Most evenings we sat in our rooms, working away with the thin plaster walls between us. Conversation was easy. Sometimes we sang. The singing was Arthur's idea. His voice was smooth and pleasant and he knew all the hits, but his great gift was for infallible harmony. However badly I carried the tune, Arthur could so accept and modulate my errors that we always sounded good, a partnership of deliberate melodies. And as our time passed by, we got better. Arthur began to speak almost daily of his wild ambition for us to become a professional act, to stand in the dim and changing lights, dressed in tuxedos, singing "How Deep is the Ocean," "Blue Moon," "My Funny Valentine," "Stardust," other standards from our long repertoire. I used to listen to him, but I knew it was fantasy.

He was my friend; we shared our money, our time, our work; we supported each other through the little communal storms which blew up occasionally. At the end we shook hands and parted. I went off to Taunton, Arthur stayed in Birmingham and became a teacher of physical education. He was a fine athlete, the fastest sprinter in the Midland counties.

31

A year later I went back up to Arthur's wedding. He married Sally, a slim, elegant girl, taller than he. When it was time for Arthur to make his speech, he stood up, smiled, raised his glass to the guests, to his bridesmaids, and with a serious, touchingly humble gesture, to his wife. He didn't say a word; and then he sat down. Later, we watched them drive off to the airport. I haven't seen them since. We wrote to each other, Arthur and I, but the letters dribbled to a halt as time gave us other things. The Christmas cards came to an end. I never thought of Arthur Marshalsea.

Five weeks ago, when I knew I was to visit Birmingham, I asked the education people to put me in touch with him. It would be good, I thought, to see what the years had done for Arthur Marshalsea. Sometimes I remembered with a smile his escapades, could almost see him running, hunched, muscular, concentrating every yard of the way. Last night a girl who said she was Arthur's daughter telephoned me from Birmingham. I listened to the young voice, realizing that this was a girl I had not known existed. She had been born and grown into her responsibilities without my knowing she was in the world.

"Great," I said. "Nice of you to telephone. I'll be in Birmingham next week, and I'd like to see Arthur."

She told me that Arthur had been very ill. I could call, but I must not be shocked when I saw him. Unusually strong and active, playing football regularly until he was nearly fifty, Arthur had set off last Easter to walk through the Lake District and come back the length of the Pennine Way. He had planned it for months, his journeys were marked, his climbs plotted, each piece of equipment tested. The girl and her mother had watched him leave the house with his backpack and his ashplant and tramp sturdily down the road. Ten minutes later he was carried home unconscious.

"It's his heart," I said. "He's had a heart attack."

Not at all. An insidious virus, attacking his brain, had brought him down. For nine weeks he had lain in the hospital, unconscious in his white bed. His return to the world was slow and painful. For a long time he had been deaf and blind. Even now, although improving, he cannot walk unaided, he cannot feed himself. Slowly he is learning to read again. His voice is often uncontrolled and often says the wrong words, which angers him. It was shocking to think of Arthur helpless. I wrote down the address as the girl gave it to me. They live just outside Knowle, on the way into Birmingham from Warwick. I know the place. I've walked along the canal bank at Knowle and watched the wild geese sit in the fields, spoken to the patient, laconic anglers waiting for small roach to bite. It won't be difficult to find Arthur's house.

After I spoke to the girl I took a glass of whiskey and water and thought about Arthur. I went to bed, but sleep was not restful and afterward I awoke with a heavy mind.

I've been thinking of what I shall say to Arthur when I see him. I can hear already the falsely cheerful voice I shall use, the loud memories. Almost anything I say to him will remind him that he cannot walk, that his speech is gutteral and false. How can I talk to him of the game at Dudley when he pushed the ball to me and I hit it sweetly even as I was falling? Or speak of the going-down dinner when we sang "That Old Black Magic?" Frankie Smedley, too drunk to see the keys, had played for us, and the next morning he had had no memory of it at all.

The days are gone when nobody in the Midlands could run as fast as Arthur, when his voice was young and strong and he could hit any note he wanted with easy accuracy, and I'll not talk of them. I'll tell him about the Dysynni Valley, how the river begins up there in Cader Idris. I'll tell him of my time in Washington State, when the waves hit the beaches at La Push and Grayland, rolling in behind the cold fling of the Pacific spray. I'll invent Summer Cove for him, describe the silken passage of the seals, tell him of my dark, unintentional journey to Tintern.

But all the time I'm thinking of Arthur lying nine weeks in a coma, his body in its clean linen being turned at the appointed times by the brisk, compassionate nurses, being fed through sterile tubes. Where was he then? He must have been away somewhere in some solitary darkness, weightless, without senses. I imagine him moving on some dark beach, so lightly he does not disturb a grain of the sand. He can feel nothing. I should like to know where he was then; I am consumed with a curious pity for Arthur Marshalsea, his useless legs, his halting speech. I see in him a terrible general fate about which we shall know very little. The still, sad music of humanity . . . wasn't it? Sing it again, Wordsworth.

The Kingfisher

On the morning of his fourteenth birthday, James met his father in the kitchen. His father came to him and held him by the shoulders, at arm's length, and looked at him with such wry and compassionate warmth that the boy was at once convinced of the imminence of some great cataclysm. Almost the same height, they stared at each other for nearly half a minute.

"So you're fourteen," James' father said. "It seems no time since I first held you in my arms. With great trepidation and very gingerly, but I held you. And here you are, fourteen."

"That's it," James said.

"Fourteen," his father said. "Always a sad anniversary for men of our family. A sad day."

He picked up his cup of coffee walked to the window, and stared seriously over the garden. When he turned away from the window, he smiled almost shyly at James, as if they shared an enormous, obligatory knowledge—some ominous secret. "Come into the dining room with me, James," he said.

The dining room was cold and quiet. Its mahogany furniture sat solidly in place, heavy, smelling of polish. James remembered it arriving at the house when he was a small boy, sent south from his grandmother's home in Yorkshire. The room was rarely used.

"Sit down," James' father said. "It would be best if you sat down."

James sat on a hard chair. Its seat had been broken long ago and repaired with some old craftsman's adhesive. James felt with his finger the small ridge of the mend. He could see a black streak of dry glue running the length of the wood.

"How do you feel?" his father said. "We can postpone this if you don't feel up to it."

"Get on with it," James said. "Whatever it is."

"Admirably stoic," his father said. "I wish I had been as stoic when my father told me."

"Told you what?" James said.

His father didn't answer. He moved quietly into a corner of the room, and then he spoke. "James, when the men of our family reach the age of fourteen, they are thought old enough to bear a terrible knowledge. Generation after generation, from father to son, we have been told this secret, pledged to pass it on in our turn. Although what we learn has in many ways blighted our lives, made saddened men of us, we have all borne our sorrow bravely. I know you will do the same."

Oh, God, thought James, rigid on his chair, we suffer from incurable hereditary madness. All over the country my cousins, tainted and cretinous, are shut away in stone towers. We are descended shamefully and illegitimately—incestuously, probably—from some nameless criminal family. He pushed away other terrors, too hideous to think of. "Tell me," he said, his voice a croak.

His father, upright and slim and still, stood in the shadows of the room. He was remote and impersonal. His face was dark. "Remember, it is my duty to tell you this," he said. "I would willingly have spared you and kept this knowledge alone."

"Hell's flames!" yelled James, his control at an end. "Tell me!"

For a long moment, until the imagined echoes of his cry had left James' ears, his father waited. Then he spoke. "There is no Father Christmas," he said.

That had been almost two weeks ago, and James still laughed at the memory, although he had been wild with rage at first. He lay in bed listening to his father's voice through the open window, and little uncontrollable giggles made him shake. It was not yet seven o'clock, but his father was already in the garden. James knew what he was doing. He was standing among his rosebushes, encouraging and cajoling. Every morning he spoke to them, full of praise if they were flowering well, like a general before battle if he felt they could do better. James got up and looked out at his father.

The lawn carried a heavy summer dew, and the marks of his father's footsteps were clear. He had wandered all over the garden, but he stood now near the rose bed, talking quietly and fondly. James could not hear what he was saying. His father's thin shanks stuck out below his silk robe. It was a glittering paisley robe in green and blue, tied at the waist with a sash of darker color. Watching his father bend above the subservient shrubs, James thought he looked like an exotic bird, a peacock of some kind.

His father loved birds to come to his garden. He had widened the trickle of a stream that bordered this plot into two small pools, so that he could keep in comfort a pair of ancient mallards, Mr. and Mrs. Waddle. This morning, hearing the man's voice, they hopped out of the water and hurried loudly to him. Mrs. Waddle, always the braver, marched to his feet and pecked at his brown slippers. She paused to look up, her head on one side, out of a round black eye. A yard away, Mr. Waddle looked on benevolently. He was in his summer glory, his green head glossy, his speculum a trim bar of reflecting blue. James' father went off to the garage, where he kept a sack of poultry food.

It was then that a kingfisher flew in, paused above the stream, and dived. He was blue lightning, an arrow of light; his flight was electric and barbarous. He took instantly from the shallow water a small fish, stickleback or minnow, and perched on the wooden post that had held a clematis, killed by harsh frost two years back. James saw the brilliant turquoise of the bird's back, the warm chestnut breast, his sturdy beak. The kingfisher held the small fish struggling across his beak and whacked it savagely and expertly against the wood before he slid it down his throat. Then he flew, seeming to leave behind a visible echo of his flight, a streak of color. James' father came out of the garage, holding a bowl of pellets. His ducks begged and skidded before him. He had missed the whole appearance of the kingfisher.

That afternoon, because his mother had gone to Birmingham to see her sister, James went with his father to the nursing home. His father would not go alone.

"Charles Emerson, to see his mother," he said to the receptionist. "And James Emerson, to see his grandmother."

The nurse smiled at them and told them to go ahead.

The old lady lay inert in her white bed, her thin hair damp and yellowish against the pillow. James' father held her hand and spoke softly to her, but she didn't answer. Her eyes were closed. She didn't know anybody. Sometimes she had spoken, but her words were disjointed and incoherent. Now she neither spoke nor moved. James watched his father grow quiet and sad as the slow minutes passed. The small room was too hot. It smelled of sickness. The voices of boys playing tennis in the park came faintly to them. James was glad when it was time to leave.

His father drove furiously out of the car park, showering the neat red gravel behind the wheels of the car. He spun the big car roughly through Redmond Corner, his tires protesting. It was always like this. He always left the nursing home in a rage of frustration, in an agony over his mother's decay.

James tapped his father's knee. "Too fast, Dad," he said. "You'll get a ticket."

His father braked, but said nothing. For several miles he drove carefully down the road, heavy now with afternoon traffic—the cars of businessmen, files of trucks taking their loads around Oxford to Southampton.

"You see what we come to," he said at last, as if he were very tired. "You see what time brings us to. We lie insensible in strange rooms, not knowing we are alive. The tyranny of the breath keeps us going. Your grandmother has committed the crime of growing too old."

James had known these moods before. He sat at his father's side and waited for him to recover. He did not understand his father's anger and impotence. It was natural to grow old, natural for the body to wither and break; it was common mortality, the human condition. He wished very much for some comfort to bring back his usual ebullient, unpredictable father.

They stopped at the traffic lights near the Queen's Theatre. "Tell me, Holmes," James said to his father, "what do you make of that old lady on the other side of the road, dressed in black?" It was an old game of theirs, although they had not played it for a long time.

His father's head jerked about, his long neck stiff—like an old heron stalking a frog. He was smiling. "Ah," he said, "you mean the retired Irish parlormaid, Watson? With a ne'er-do-well son in the army and a pipe-smoking husband?"

"Holmes," James said, "you astound me! How on earth did you gather that information? Do you know the woman?"

"Never saw her before in my life," his father said. "But you know my methods, Watson. I knew she was a parlormaid because her right arm is six inches longer than her left—the result, Watson, of many years of carrying heavy buckets of coal to the upstairs parlors in which her employers sat."

James laughed, turning in his seat to look at his father. "Good gracious, Holmes," he said. "You do astound me. Go on."

"A mere nothing," his father said. "I know she is retired because, apart from her evident maturity, she would not be about so early in the evening were she still employed. And as she is still wearing, although St. Patrick's Day is long past, a bunch of faded shamrock at her collar, she is undoubtedly Irish."

"When you put it like that, Holmes, it's quite simple," James said. "But what about her son in the army and her pipe-smoking husband? I have you there, I think."

"Not at all," said his father. He was well into the game now, his gloom forgotten. "The shamrock is fastened to her coat by an old brooch, on which the word *Mother* is clearly to be discerned. The parcel she carries is addressed to a private in the infantry named McCarthy. It is safe to assume he is her son. That he is a ne'er-do-well is evident from the woman's dress. No decent son would allow his mother to go out so shabbily garbed."

"Great," James said. "Pretty good. What about the husband?"

"That," said his father with relish, "is the easiest deduction of all. Did you not observe that the woman's clothes are spotted all over with tiny burns, small marks of scorching? They prove beyond all doubt that she has spent many years in the close vicinity of a man who is a careless pipe-smoker, undoubtedly her husband."

"A full score," said James. "You haven't lost your skill."

His father took the car past a row of parked vehicles outside the library. "Your turn," he said. "Tell me, Holmes, what do you make of the sinister-looking man who stands outside the filling station?"

"You mean," James said, "the ex-sailor who subsequently became a policeman, was dismissed for taking bribes, and now earns a casual living as a gardener?"

"Holmes," said his father, "you astonish me."

They ate supper together, silently, contentedly, and afterward James walked in the garden. The evening was still warm, and Mr. and Mrs. Waddle muttered from their stream. High up, the seagulls were trailing their irregular columns back to the beach. A little tatter of silk, oriental in its brilliance, had blown from somewhere onto the lawn. James bent over it. It was the kingfisher. He picked it up, and it lay dead on his hand, light as dust. Its head rolled loosely of its own tiny weight, as if its neck were broken. James examined the short, blunt wings, touched the dry beak.

From the house his father began to sing. "*Questa o quella,*" he sang, his voice breaking comically on the higher notes, "*per me pari sono.*"

James held the dead bird on his open palm. He carried it to the long grass beneath the maple tree in the corner of the garden. He placed the bird in the dark grass behind the tree and stood above it, rubbing his hands together briskly. He would not tell his father about the kingfisher, not about its vivid morning flight across the garden, not about its small, irrevocable death. He would spare his father that knowledge.

My Uncle's Story

Sometimes my uncle drank too much. Ordinarily a morose man, silent, possessed altogether by a refined melancholy, his single gesture toward speech would normally be a sigh of the slightest possible audibility, an exhalation as soft as the air on which it floated. He was a still, downcast man, hunched in his corner, effaced by sadness.

But when he drank too much his eyes grew fierce, his speech blossomed and became oracular, the dark fancies of his usual gloom grew ripe and colorful. I saw this transfiguration only once, when I was ten years old. Returning late from a school concert where I and other boys had sung a number of roaring songs in which the brave Welsh had swung their swords around the musical battlefields, I called on my way home at my grandmother's house. My uncle, a bachelor, lived with her. He was her oldest son. I went into the back room and there was my uncle, upright and luminous, enthroned on his wooden armchair. He looked marvelous.

I told my grandmother about the concert, how Jackie Colbert had dived through a hoop during the gymnastic display, tumbled awkwardly, and broken his collarbone, how Ronnie Protheroe had imitated a duck and a horse, and I sang for her the opening lines of the most patriotic of our songs. She was well pleased and gave me the crust of a new loaf, a piece of mild cheese, and a glass of milk.

Of all this my uncle seemed oblivious. He sat upright in his chair, his face fiery, smiling. He nodded occasionally as if he could hear conversations unheard by us. Serenely contemptuous of all around him, he dispensed favors to invisible favorites, dismissed invisible peasants with a wave of his hand. I looked at him with delight.

"What's the matter with him?" I asked my grandmother. "Is he drunk?"

"He's merry," my grandmother said. "We might say he's merry."

My uncle turned royally toward us and spoke.

"Do you think," he said, in rich and jocular tones, "that the world was made in jest?"

"Stop it, Wil," said my grandmother comfortably. She was darning a gray woolen sock and had her steel-rimmed glasses on. My uncle didn't hear her.

"Read where you will," my uncle said, indicating a long horizon of learning and study with the flat of his hand. "Read the Bible, the Koran, read where you will. But the creatures of air and water have a separate wisdom."

I thought about this. It seemed reasonable.

"That's enough, Wil," my grandmother said. "You'll frighten the boy."

"I'm not frightened," I said.

My uncle looked at me. His eyes were glittering and ecstatic.

"Don't be afraid, boy," he said sharply.

"I'm not afraid," I said.

"Remember," cried my uncle in a great voice, "tall gods walk the earth, but their feet are in the mud!"

He stood up and raised his arms above his head.

Great stuff, I thought, going home at a trot, leaping the wet ditch every fifth stride. Sometimes I missed and fell in.

"Where have you been until now; look at your boots!" said my mother, in a crescendo of disbelief.

I looked at my boots. The ditch had been pretty dirty. I had left a plain trail all down the hall.

"Remember," I said sternly, "great gods walk the earth, but their feet are in the mud."

"What are you talking about?" my mother said. As I passed her she landed a grim slap to the back of my head and I staggered into the kitchen. She followed me. I could see she was intrigued.

"Where did you hear such rubbish?" she said.

"Uncle Wil told me," I said, "and also about the creatures of air and water. They have a different wisdom."

"Oh, him," she said. "Been drinking, has he? I hope you don't take after him, that's all."

I went to bed.

My uncle Wil hadn't always been melancholy. He was spry and sociable as a young man. Once, my father told me, my uncle had gone out with Elvet Parry and they had become famously drunk.

"Oh, they made a proper job of it," my father said, slapping his knee with delight as he remembered my uncle's adventure.

My uncle and Elvet Parry had always been friends. As boys they had walked to Cardiff and, adding sufficient years to their ages, joined the army. This was during the Great War. They had been private soldiers in the fifth battalion of the Welsh Regiment, an infantry regiment, and fought in France until the last day of hostilities. When they finally returned home they were still only eighteen years old. They worked together in the local colliery. Most Friday evenings they met, pooled their money, and set off on a tour of the public houses in our village and in villages nearby. This is what they had done one winter Friday before I was born.

They began, as they always did, at the Wheatsheaf, a quiet, serious inn near my grandmother's house. Here my uncle and Elvet Parry spoke to some of their friends, talking slowly and gently, their voices hardly louder than the click of dominoes. The Wheatsheaf was a great place for dominoes. Relaxed, easy, the week's work in the past, the friends then began to visit, in reeling succession, The Dynevor Arms, The George, The Barley Mow, and The Greyhound. After this they left the village and made for The Blue Boar, a small tavern in the hills where the landlord was a friend of theirs, and where little regard was paid to the lawful hours of drinking. At midnight all the

revelers were turned out. Sentimental fathers, wavering a little and very happy, went home to their wives and children.
But my uncle and Elvet Parry, without such responsibilities,
tottered into the night. Each carried two bottles of whiskey,
purchased as an afterthought from Dennis Montague, landlord
of The Blue Boar.

"They could stand, then," Mr. Montague told my father.
"Oh, yes, they could stand all right. With help, of course."

It had begun to snow, a fine dry snow with flakes small
and pointed as needles. Hard particles of blown snow found
the least crack between the slates of roofs and heaped themselves in frozen pyramids on the attic floors; they crept in drifts
under the doors of houses, dying in leaking streams as the warm
air hit them; they powdered the lanes and streets and fields
with a glittering dust. It was very cold.

In the early hours of the morning the Griffiths boys, coming home from a dance in the town, saw my uncle and Elvet
standing under the lamp that lit the village square. They stood
close together and they were singing. They were singing, the
Griffiths boys said, the songs of the dead war: "Mademoiselle
from Armentieres," "Tipperary," "Keep the Home Fires Burning," "Pack Up Your Troubles." And as Desmond Griffiths cautiously unlocked his door, taking infinite care not to wake his
father, Elvet Parry began a performance of rich nostalgia.

"Honest," Desmond said, "it was enough to make you cry."

"There's a long, long trail a-winding," sang Elvet Parry, "into
the land of my dreams." And soft as a puff Desmond and Arnold
Griffiths shut their heavy door and locked the singing out. That
was the last anyone saw or heard of Elvet Parry and my uncle
for two days.

The bitter weather kept everyone indoors. A few brave
women scurried to the shops, a few hardy children played in
the light, unsatisfactory snow. It was an astonishment when,
late that evening, my grandmother marched into my parents'
house. She was wrapped in her thickest coat, a long scarf was
wound about her head and fastened under her chin.

"Wil hasn't been home," she said. "He didn't come home
last night. I don't know where he is."

"Don't worry, Mum," my mother said, "he'll be holed up in some bar with Elvet Parry, not a leg between the two of them. Oh, a fine brother, he is. A fine name we'll have in the village with that pair."

"I called at the Parry house as I came here," my grandmother said. "Elvet hasn't been home either. I spoke to his sister, Mavis. She's worried sick."

"Men," my mother said. "They don't think."

"They bought two loaves and a large tin of corned beef," my grandmother said, "knocked Mr. Willis up until he came down to the shop and served them. One o'clock in the morning."

"Did they, now," said my father.

He took my grandmother home and then he went all round the village, speaking to his friends, mustering the young men. The next morning, at first light, the men met, grumbling and laughing, gloved to the elbows, muffled in clothes. They set out for the hills, moving quickly at first, and then, as they met the first steep, more slowly, calling to each other to keep in touch, poking their sticks into drifts, whistling their dogs. All day they climbed, finding nothing. By mid-afternoon it was almost dark. Snow began to fall, in heavy flakes. It was lovely, my father said, to see the line of torches strung along the hill, to hear the men call to each other through the falling dark. Subtly the snow altered familiar contours: the bleak slopes were swept and dark, the hollows filled and hidden by whipped drifts. At last they faced the erratic rim of granite which forms the summit of our mountain. Fissured and broken, it had been ground to its stubborn core by centuries of bitter weather. There they found Elvet Parry, at bay against a slab of rock. He stood on guard in the swirling fall, facing his friends as they climbed toward him.

"Halt!" he cried. "Who goes there?"

"It's all right, Elvet," my father said. "We're the relief party. You can stand down now."

"Thank God you've come, sergeant," said Elvet. "Private Thomas is in the dugout, badly wounded."

"We'll look after him," my father said. "Take Private Parry down the line, men."

45

My uncle was in a cave behind Elvet Parry's watchpost. He was heavily asleep and wounded by whiskey. Turn and turn about, the befuddled comrades had been on guard in the confused hills, thinking they were again at war. They were taken home and put to bed, hot bottles at their feet, their curtains drawn against any intrusion of curiosity. They were quite unharmed. The next day they strode about the smiling village like returned warriors, like heroes.

"They have no sense of shame," said my mother, bitterly, as she watched their triumphant progress.

But I delighted in this story and would ask my father to tell it at least once a week.

"How did you know where to find them?" I asked my father.

"It was the bully beef and bread," my father explained. "They had drawn their rations, exactly as they had when in the army, so I knew they'd got confused and thought they were back in France. After that it was just a matter of deciding where they'd hole up."

"I don't know how you can be so tolerant," my mother said, "and you a teetotaler. I'd have given them France."

"They had a bad war," my father said stoutly. "You don't forget the war. It's there, behind your life, every day. And your training is always part of you. They were good infantrymen." He was a soldier by instinct as well as by training. His mind was filled with the great battles of his life, Mons, Verdun, Salonika, the Dardanelles. He wore always in the lapel of his jacket the miniature ribbons of his medals, and every man who had fought in the Great War was his comrade-in-arms and his friend; he would defend such a man to the end.

When I could walk far enough my father took me to see the cave in which they had found my sleeping uncle. In my imagination I had seen an echoing vast of darkness, a vaulted black cathedral where a pygmy uncle slept against a flat of basalt; but it was no more than a disappointing cleft in the stone, sheltered enough to turn a wind, long enough for a man to stretch comfortably. When I saw it, two sheep occupied it. They stared at me out of their skulls with malevolent yellow eyes, and I hurried back to my father.

Oh, he was nimble and happy enough when he was young, was my uncle. I can remember him as a young man, I can just remember him. We were in my grandmother's garden and he was dancing and grinning at me. His boots were brilliantly polished and I could see the gleaming toe caps advancing toward me, prancing away. He strutted on his toes, lifting his knees high, and held a shilling between thumb and forefinger. His face was pink and mischievous; he wriggled his devils' eyebrows at me. I was terrified.

"Say it," he wheedled. "Say it, like a good boy, and you shall have this lovely shilling."

But I stood mute in the bean rows and would not utter the blasphemous word he wanted me to repeat. My mother leaned scornfully against the wall of the house, confident of my perfect innocence. I was very small.

"He won't say it," she said, "not if you offer him a pound note."

"Oh, Wil won't do that," my grandmother said. "I don't like admitting such a thing about my own son, but he won't put a pound note at risk. I'm surprised at him waving that shilling about. Wil isn't generous."

My uncle laughed, stood up straight, and ran down the lane, in and out of the shadows. He was lithe enough then.

When the depression hit our valley and the collieries closed, my uncle lost his job. He took it hard. Each day, as I walked to school, I used to pass small groups of workless men on the village square. They spoke quietly to each other, seldom laughed, were united in strong bonds of friendship by a common hardship. But my uncle was never among them. He grew restless and bad-tempered; he walked the mountain paths for hours. One morning, calling at my grandmother's, I saw she had been crying.

"What's the matter, Gran?" I said. "Where's Uncle Wil?" But she didn't answer. She gave me a bacon sandwich and hurried me off to school. That evening my mother said that my uncle had packed a few belongings and marched away. He had walked away to look for work in some other place and nobody knew where he was.

"He's just a tramp," my mother said, "a common tramp. I never thought he'd come to this." But she sounded very sad.

I became accustomed to my grandmother living on her own in her scrubbed house. I grew accustomed to her long silences as she sat in her chair. When I told her about the drama and injustices of my life at school, she didn't laugh anymore, or ask questions.

"Jimmie Sullivan fell off the playground wall," I said, "and one of the big boys wheeled him home in a barrow."

"That's nice," my grandmother said, not listening at all.

I nearly forgot about my uncle. If I thought of him, I imagined him as a tramp, a man of great panache and cunning. I knew from my reading that tramps carried their food in red bandannas tied to the ends of sticks and slung arrogantly over their shoulders. They had infinite freedom. They lit fires at the sides of roads and boiled their kettles; they drank from tin cups and slept, carefree, in barns. They shaved rarely, they wore huge boots with holes in the rough leather, they set snares for unsuspecting rabbits. I imagined my uncle such a man, but when I came to think of his face I couldn't remember it. I admired the romance of his life.

One day a letter came for my grandmother. In it my uncle said he was well and hoped all was well at home. There was no address. My grandmother and I pored over the postmark. The round impression was dark and indistinct, but together we decided the letter had been posted in Doncaster.

"Doncaster," said my father, when I told him, and he unfolded his road map of Great Britain. It covered half the big kitchen table.

"Here it is," my father said, putting the tip of his finger on Doncaster. "It's on the Great North Road, he's walking the Great North Road."

I looked with satisfaction at the bold, unswerving line of the Great North Road as it moved up the map from London, over the marks of folding, on and on. Nothing could stop it. The Great North Road! I thought of its unimaginable distances, I saw in my mind the great arc of its skies, I imagined my indomitable uncle, smaller than a fly, tramping on, day after day, up the face of England.

"Poor old Wil," my mother said. "I feel for him, sleeping in doss houses."

Years later, when I was nine years old and rough and noisy and prepared to utter blasphemous words without any payment at all, my uncle came home. He returned during the two summer weeks when I was at Barry Island with my parents, and he was established, hunched and silent, in his corner when I saw him.

"That's your Uncle Wil," my grandmother said. "Say hullo to him."

"Hullo," I said. He sat unmoving in his chair, one thin leg crossed over the other, inert, long hands resting in his lap. I couldn't even see him breathe.

He looked at me quickly from under the white lids of his eyes and quickly away. I regarded him with the greatest thoroughness. He did not look like a tramp. He was neither jolly nor carefree and he was flawlessly clean. I had never seen such a clean man. It seemed as if he had used up all his allowable grime and squalor in his years on the road, and no speck of dust would ever settle on him again. His shirt, his black boots, the skin of his face and of his thin arms, for he wore his shirtsleeves rolled, were all gleaming. I did not recognize him. He was an old man. His hair was sparse and colorless, his narrow face deeply lined. He was very thin. I could see the bones of his face. His bold nose was cleanly and delicately formed and two deep lines ran down from the edges of his nostrils. His lips were pale and delicate, turned down in an expression at once resigned and infinitely sad. During the whole time I was there he seemed never to move. I had expected a great, beaming, winking man, a man who took what he wanted from society with a broad smile and a swaggering touch of the forelock. I found it hard to believe in this silent, hygienic man. Later, I heard him speak to my grandmother. His voice was harsh and brusque, and he kept his words to the minimum. It hurt me to hear him speak to her, it seemed as if he were giving orders to her, but she didn't mind. When he walked he found it difficult to straighten his shoulders, and his feet were hard as clubs. He hobbled along, bent and anxious, with short, painful steps. And after a while, since he never spoke to me, I ignored him altogether. Every Christmas I bought him a cigar. He would take my dutiful gift, unwrap it, roll it in his long fingers, pass it under his nose. Then he'd smile and nod. The memory of the one splendid moment when he told me about the great gods who walk the earth stayed with me, but I was never to have it repeated.

One Saturday, the day I played for the school first team, I called at my grandmother's on my way home from the match. I was tall now, had a man's voice, was an aristocrat in the school community. I carried my football jersey openly, a badge of my rank and fame.

"That's a pretty jersey," my grandmother said. "I always liked black and gold, a lovely combination."

"The first-team colors," I said, offhandedly.

"The first team!" she said, splendidly impressed. She waved a hand at my uncle. "Wil," she said, "was never keen on football. Cricket was Wil's game. Wasn't it, Wil."

The old man stirred, twisting his bent shoulders against the fabric of his shirt.

"Yes," he said. "It was. I liked cricket. I was a good player." His voice was rough and challenging, as if we had been scornful of his ability.

"He used to play a lot of cricket," my grandmother said. "Oh, those white flannel trousers. The trouble I used to have getting the grass stains off."

I couldn't believe he had ever played any game in his life.

"I was a batsman," my uncle said. "I've still got my bat. I keep it in the wardrobe in my room."

"That's good," I said. I wasn't too interested. When my grandmother took her basket to go down to the butcher's, I offered to go for her.

"No," she said, "I have to give old Millward a bit of my eloquence. The lamb he sent up last week must have been born several years ago. I've never known such meat. He needs keeping up to the mark."

She went out through the front door, always a sign of seriousness in my grandmother. Normally we travelled through the back door and down the garden path. I picked up the paper and began to read. I was whistling.

"Do you want to see that cricket bat?" my uncle said. He startled me.

"I don't mind," I said. His voice was still rough, but there was something in it that made me look up from my reading. I saw that he really wanted to show me his cricket bat. He sat on the edge of his chair, eager as a child.

"Go on, then," I said, "let's see this famous bat."

He went upstairs and I could hear him open the door of his room. He came down with an old bat and a pair of white cricket boots. The boots were immaculate, without stain, the laces clean and fresh. My uncle put them down on the floor.

"They're good boots," he said. "I clean them up twice a year. I like to keep them nice."

He must have had them for twenty years or more. They were laughable old boots; I'd never seen anything so old-fashioned.

"Yes, they're lovely boots," my uncle said. "So flexible. I couldn't get them on now. My feet are so stiff."

He handed me the bat. It was very heavy and the handle was unusually long. Some of the whipping had come away from the handle and it snapped when I pulled it. All its strength had gone.

"It needs oiling," my uncle said. "It needs a drop of oil, a good rub of linseed oil, then put it away for a fortnight, then a good treatment of linseed again. It would be fine then, sweet as a nut."

The blade was dark brown with age, and pocked on the surface where it had struck cricket balls in matches long before I was born. It was so dry that the skin of the wood was beginning to lift in little shields, in thin patches, away from the body of the blade.

"You can have it," he said, "if you want it."

I knew he didn't want me to have it. He fussed about, reaching toward the bat as I turned it in my hands. The bat was finished, old and dry. It would break at the first stroke.

"I don't play cricket," I said. "It would be no use to me. But it's a good bat." *Be generous,* I thought.

He took the old bat from me and held it with the greatest gentleness.

"The first time I used it," he said, "I scored fifty-seven with it. The first time I ever used it."

I saw with surprise that he was very happy. He stroked the flaking wood with his hand and he was smiling.

"Uncle," I said, "what was it like when you were a tramp?"

For the life of me, I don't know why I said it. It wasn't in my head at all, and I was astonished when the words came out.

"It wasn't bad, sometimes," my uncle answered.

"Why did you go?" I asked him. "What made you just walk away?"

"You don't remember it," he said. "You don't remember what it was like. You're too young. But I remember day after day with nothing to do, no work, unused. Two years I was like that. I used to get up in the morning, wash and shave, get dressed, walk up to the library, read magazines six months old. Meaningless. In the afternoon I'd walk the hills, come home, sit here staring at the fire, go to bed. Every day without dignity or purpose."

"I remember men standing about on the square," I said.

"There were plenty like me in Wales," my uncle said, "young men, rotting away. But that isn't the real reason I left. There was something in me, oh, a wish to see what was over the horizon, I suppose. And it grew and grew until it was a great lump in my chest. There was no denying it. One morning I got up and I knew I had to go. I walked away, travelling light. I had nothing to carry. Your grandmother cried, but she didn't try to stop me. I marched up the valley and over Dowlais Top, and I'd never felt so free in all my life. It was as if the whole of my days had just been preparation for this, as if the air and the light and the short grass of the mountain were all mine, I owned them all."

My uncle's voice had grown young and pliant. His blue eyes were shining. He watched himself, straight and youthful, step out of the past and walk for our inspection.

"I did well at first," he said. "Picked apples and hops in Hereford. It was good, working in the hop fields. Poor people came out of South Wales and Birmingham, whole families, grandmothers, parents, children, their dogs and cats. It was like a holiday for them. We lived in camps, and everywhere there was the rich smell of the hops, on your hands, on your clothes, in the air. I was very happy then, in Hereford."

He was smiling, he held his head high.

"I worked with a boy from near Swansea," my uncle said, "about twenty, two or three years younger than I was. Told me his name was Terry. But names mean nothing, not on the road. You throw your name away and somebody gives you another."

"And what was your name, Uncle?" I asked him.

"It doesn't matter," he said. "Sometimes I had one name, sometimes another."

I waited without moving for him to go on.

"We worked together," my uncle said, "Terry and I. We were casual laborers in Gloucester and Wiltshire, digging ditches, breaking stones, doing whatever came our way. We didn't earn very much, but we were eating, living. Thin! You've never seen two such thin boys. Well, I never seemed to have much muscle. Terry looked worse because he was a tall boy. We worked together and we tramped together, shared what we had. We were both boys from the valleys. We travelled through Devizes toward the end of autumn, and the nights were getting cold. We did what we could, helped on market days, driving cattle. Some farmers gave us a copper or two, but times were hard for them. We chopped wood. We had a week planting young trees on a hillside, young fir trees. That was good. We kept travelling east, bit by bit. We weren't making for anywhere in particular. Some said that there was work in Slough. Perhaps we were making for Slough."

Imperceptibly, my uncle's voice had grown slow and sad. It was as if he were speaking an elegy which he alone had preserved from the wastes of time. There was something almost ceremonial about his speech, as if what he had to say were long rehearsed, familiar to him.

"We had a hard time of it," he said, "once the winter came. And Terry worse than I did. He was such a tall thin lad. It was the rain mostly, the rain that beat us. The dry cold was not

so bad. We were in Oxford on Christmas Day. We were singing in the streets by then, begging. I was ashamed to sing, but
Terry didn't mind. He'd stand in the gutter and lift his head
and sing, as naturally as if he were in his own kitchen. I would
hold my cap out to people passing by. We didn't make much
money. And the police were very difficult, they moved us on
pretty roughly. I think we were light-headed by then, with cold
and hunger.''

My uncle sat in his chair and held himself hunched against
the remembered cold.

"At the last," he said, "we were somewhere between Wood-
stock and Bicester. I didn't rightly know what a state we were
in. It was January, early in January, and the wind was killing
everything before it. I could see the big fires we kept in the
house, and smell beef roasting in the oven. I looked up at the
stars in a sky without any help in it at all. I'd never seen anything so cold in all my days. There was no shelter anywhere.
We came around a bend in that forsaken road and we saw a
stack of big pipes, ready for laying new drains. They were about
fourteen feet long. I put an old sack over the windy end of
one, and we crawled in. I went to sleep at once, never stirred.
Oh, I was tired. In the morning, when I woke up, I couldn't
rouse Terry. I shouted at him, tugged him. He was dead. Thin,
hard, frozen to the pipe. I couldn't move him. I didn't know
what to do. Nobody passed. There weren't many cars about
then. In the end, I walked away. I didn't look back. I didn't
tell anybody. What could I do? I didn't know his name, I didn't
know his address, where he came from, if he had a family.''

I saw in my uncle's eyes an old sadness. Troubled, griev-
ing, he stared beyond me at the tragedy of his friend's death.
He turned away, leaning back in his chair in his former defeated
attitude, as if it were the shape into which his body, accustomed
by long usage, naturally fell.

"What could I have done?" he said. His voice was resigned
and exhausted, his speech a statement of his failure.

"I don't know, Uncle," I said, but he didn't hear me. He
sat limp in his chair, his face turned away, his hands flat on
the blade of his old bat. He was so frail that I knew I couldn't

have touched him, even to comfort him. I stood up. The pale skin of his scalp looked silver in the afternoon light.

I picked up my jersey and walked out into the garden. The last of the string beans hung on their sticks, together with the longest pods which my grandmother saved to form her next year's seeds. Very long now, heavy, they were brown and dry, swollen at intervals as the seeds grew within. I walked down the path and into the lane. And I began to run, I ran as if released, I ran with ferocity down the lane, in and out of the shadows, I ran faster than I had ever run before.

Blackberries

Mr. Frensham opened his shop at eight-thirty, but it was past nine when the woman and the child went in. The shop was empty and there were no foot-marks on the fresh sawdust shaken onto the floor. The child listened to the melancholy sound of the bell as the door closed behind him and he scuffed his feet in the yellow sawdust. Underneath, the boards were brown and worn, and dark knots stood up in them. He had never been in this shop before. He was going to have his hair cut for the first time in his life, except for the times when his mother had trimmed it gently behind his neck.

Mr. Frensham was sitting in a large chair, reading a newspaper. He could make the chair turn around, and he spun twice about in it before he put down his paper, smiled, and said, "Good morning."

He was an old man, thin, with flat white hair. He wore a white coat.

"One gentleman," he said, "to have his locks shorn."

He put a board across the two arms of his chair, lifted the child, and sat him on it.

"How are you, my dear? And your father, is he well?" he said to the child's mother.

He took a sheet from a cupboard on the wall and wrapped it about the child's neck, tucking it into his collar. The sheet covered the child completely and hung almost to the floor. Cautiously the boy moved his hidden feet. He could see the bumps they made in the cloth. He moved his finger against the inner surface of the sheet and made a six with it, and then an eight. He liked those shapes.

"Snip snip," said Mr. Frensham, "and how much does the gentleman want off? All of it? All his lovely curls? I think not."

"Just an ordinary cut, please, Mr. Frensham," said the child's mother, "not too much off. I, my husband and I, we thought it was time for him to look like a little boy. His hair grows so quickly."

Mr. Frensham's hands were very cold. His hard fingers turned the boy's head first to one side and then to the other and the boy could hear the long scissors snapping away behind him, and above his ears. He was quite frightened, but he liked watching the small tufts of his hair drop lightly on the sheet which covered him, and then roll an inch or two before they stopped. Some of the hair fell to the floor and by moving his hand surreptitiously he could make nearly all of it fall down. The hair fell without a sound. Tilting his head slightly, he could see the little bunches on the floor, not belonging to him any more.

"Easy to see who this boy is," Mr. Frensham said to the child's mother, "I won't get redder hair in the shop today. Your father had hair like this when he was young, very much this color. I've cut your father's hair for fifty years. He's keeping well, you say? There, I think that's enough. We don't want him to dislike coming to see me."

He took the sheet off the child and flourished it hard before folding it and putting it on a shelf. He swept the back of the child's neck with a small brush. Nodding his own old head in admiration, he looked at the child's hair for flaws in the cutting.

"Very handsome," he said.

The child saw his face in a mirror. It looked pale and large, but also much the same as always. When he felt the back of his neck, the new short hairs stood up sharp against his hand.

"We're off to do some shopping," his mother said to Mr. Frensham as she handed him the money.

58

They were going to buy the boy a cap, a round cap with a little button on top and a peak over his eyes, like his cousin Harry's cap. The boy wanted the cap very much. He walked seriously beside his mother and he was not impatient even when she met Mrs. Lewis and talked to her, and then took a long time at the fruiterer's buying apples and potatoes.

"This is the smallest size we have," the man in the clothes shop said. "It may be too large for him."

"He's just had his hair cut," said his mother. "That should make a difference."

The man put the cap on the boy's head and stood back to look. It was a beautiful cap. The badge in front was shaped like a shield and it was red and blue. It was not too big, although the man could put two fingers under it, at the side of the boy's head.

"On the other hand, we don't want it too tight," the man said. "We want something he can grow into, something that will last him a long time."

"Oh, I hope so," his mother said. "It's expensive enough."

The boy carried the cap himself, in a brown paper bag that had "Price, Clothiers, High Street" on it. He could read it all except "Clothiers" and his mother told him that. They put his cap, still in its bag, in a drawer when they got home.

His father came home late in the afternoon. The boy heard the firm clap of the closing door and his father's long step down the hall. He leaned against his father's knee while the man ate his dinner. The meal had been keeping warm in the oven and the plate was very hot. A small steam was rising from the potatoes, and the gravy had dried to a thin crust where it was shallow at the side of the plate. The man lifted the dry gravy with his knife and fed it to his son, very carefully lifting it into the boy's mouth, as if he were feeding a small bird. The boy loved this. He loved the hot savor of his father's dinner, the way his father cut away small delicacies for him and fed them to him slowly. He leaned drowsily against his father's leg.

Afterwards he put on his cap and stood before his father, certain of the man's approval. The man put his hand on the boy's head and looked at him without smiling.

"On Sunday," he said, "we'll go for a walk. Just you and I. We'll be men together."

Although it was late in September, the sun was warm and the paths dry. The man and his boy walked beside the disused canal and powdery white dust covered their shoes. The boy thought of the days before he had been born, when the canal had been busy. He thought of the long boats pulled by solid horses, gliding through the water. In his head he listened to the hushed, wet noises they would have made, the soft waves slapping the banks, and green tench looking up as the barges moved above them, their water suddenly darkened. His grandfather had told him about that. But now the channel was filled with mud and tall reeds. Bullrush and watergrass grew in the damp passages. He borrowed his father's ashplant and knocked the heads off a company of seeding dandelions, watching the tiny parachutes carry away their minute dark burdens.

"There they go," he said to himself. "There they go, sailing away to China."

"Come on," said his father, "or we'll never reach Fletcher's Woods."

The boy hurried after his father. He had never been to Fletcher's Woods. Once his father had heard a nightingale there. It had been in the summer, long ago, and his father had gone with his friends, to hear the singing bird. They had stood under a tree and listened. Then the moon went down and his father, stumbling home, had fallen into a blackberry bush.

"Will there be blackberries?" he asked.

"There should be," his father said. "I'll pick some for you."

In Fletcher's Wood there was shade beneath the trees, and sunlight, thrown in yellow patches on to the grass, seemed to grow out of the ground rather than come from the sky. The boy stepped from sunlight to sunlight, in and out of shadow. His father showed him a tangle of bramble, hard with thorns, its leaves just beginning to color into autumn, its long runners dry and brittle on the grass. Clusters of purple fruit hung in the branches. His father reached up and chose a blackberry for him. Its skin was plump and shining, each of its purple globes held a point of reflected light.

"You can eat it," his father said.

The boy put the blackberry in his mouth. He rolled it with his tongue, feeling its irregularity, and crushed it against the roof of his mouth. Released juice, sweet and warm as summer, ran down his throat, hard seeds cracked between his teeth. When he laughed his father saw that his mouth was deeply stained. Together they picked and ate the dark berries, until their lips were purple and their hands marked and scratched.

"We should take some for your mother," the man said.

He reached with his stick and pulled down high canes where the choicest berries grew, picking them to take home. They had nothing to carry them in, so the boy put his new cap on the grass and they filled its hollow with berries. He held the cap by its edges and they went home.

"It was a stupid thing to do," his mother said, "utterly stupid. What were you thinking of?"

The young man did not answer.

"If we had the money, it would be different," his mother said. "Where do you think the money comes from?"

"I know where the money comes from," his father said. "I work hard enough for it."

"His new cap," his mother said. "How am I to get him another?"

The cap lay on the table and by standing on tiptoe the boy could see it. Inside it was wet with the sticky juice of blackberries. Small pieces of blackberry skins were stuck to it. The stains were dark and irregular.

"It will probably dry out all right," his father said.

His mother's face was red and distorted, her voice shrill.

"If you had anything like a job," she shouted, "and could buy caps by the dozen, then—"

She stopped and shook her head. His father turned away, his mouth hard.

"I do what I can," he said.

"That's not much!" his mother said. She was tight with scorn. "You don't do much!"

Appalled, the child watched the quarrel mount and spread.

He began to cry quietly, to himself, knowing that it was a different weeping to any he had experienced before, that he was crying for a different pain. And the child began to understand that they were different people; his father, his mother, himself, and that he must learn sometimes to be alone.

The Wind,
The Cold Wind

I was almost at the top of Victoria Road, under the big maroon boarding advertising Camp Coffee, when I heard Jimmy James shouting.

"Hey Ginger!" he shouted. "Hold on a minute, Ginger!"

He couldn't wait to reach me. He ran across the road in front of the Cardiff bus as if it didn't exist. There he was, large, red-faced, rolling urgently along like a boy with huge, slow springs in his knees, like a boy heaving himself through heavy, invisible water. Jimmy couldn't read very well. Once I'd written a letter for him, to his sister who lived in Birmingham and worked in a chocolate factory; once he'd let me walk to school with him and other large, important boys. He stopped in front of me, weighty, impassable.

"I heard you were dead," he said. "The boys told me you were dead."

His large brown eyes looked down at me accusingly.

"Not me, Jim," I said. "Never felt fitter, Jim."

He thought that too sprightly by half. His fat cheeks reddened and he wagged a finger at me. It looked as thick as a club.

"Watch it, Ginge," he said.

He was fifteen years old, five years older than I, and big. He was a boy to be feared. I slowed it.

"No, Jim," I said smiling soberly, "I'm not dead."

"The boys told me you were," he said.

He was looking at me with the utmost care, his whole attitude reproachful and disappointed. I was immediately guilty. I had let Jimmy James down, I could see that. And then, in an instant, I understood, for something very like this had happened to me before.

The previous winter, in January, a boy called Tony Plumley had drowned in a pond on the mountain. I'd spent a lot of time worrying about Tony Plumley. The unready ice had split beneath him and tumbled him into the darkness. For weeks afterwards, lying in my bed at night, I'd followed him down, hearing him choke, feeling the stiffening chill of the water. I had watched his skin turn blue as ice, I had felt his lungs fill to the throat with suffocating water, known the moment when at last his legs had gone limp and boneless. I had given Tony Plumley all the pity and fear I possessed. And later, in irresistible terror, I had gone with him into his very grave. Then, one day when I had forgotten all about him and was running carefree along a dappled path in the summer woods, there he was, in front of me, Tony Plumley, alive. I thought of all that sympathetic terror spent and wasted and I was wildly angry. I charged him with being drowned.

"It wasn't me," Tony Plumley said, backing off fast.

"It was you," I said. "Put up your fists."

But Tony Plumley stood still and cautious outside the range of my eager jabs. Taking the greatest care, speaking slowly, he explained that he was not drowned at all, that he had never been sliding on the pond, that his mother would not have let him. It was another boy, Tony Powell, who had dropped through the cheating ice and died. I had been confused by the similarity of their names. I stood there trying to reconcile myself to a world in which the firm certainty of death had proved unfaithful, a world in which Tony Powell, a boy unknown to me, was suddenly dead. Perplexed, I dropped my avenging hands.

"Get moving, Plumley," I said.

He slid tactfully past me and thumped away down the path.

So I knew exactly how Jimmy James felt. I'd used a lot of emotion on Plumley and Jim must have been imagining my death with much the same intensity. I understood his disappointment, deserved his reproach, stood resignedly under his just anger. I knew, too, how the confusion had come about.

"It's not me, Jim," I said, "it's Maldwyn Farraday. It's because we've both got red hair."

This completely baffled Jim. He looked at me in despair.

"What's red hair got to do with it?" he said loudly.

"We've both got red hair," I explained, "Maldwyn Farraday and I. And we live in the same street and we're friends. It's Maldwyn's dead. People mix us up."

Jim didn't say anything.

"I'm going to the funeral tomorrow," I said.

Jimmy James curled his lip in contempt and turned away, his heavy shoulders outraged, his scuffed shoes slapping the pavement. I waited until he had turned the corner by the delicatessen and then I ran. I ran past the shops still ablaze for the Christmas which was already gone, I ran past Davies' where unsold decorated cakes still held their blue and pink rosettes, their tiny edible skaters and Father Christmasses, their stale, festive messages in scarlet piping; I ran past Mr. Roberts' shop without looking once at his sumptuous boxes of confectionery, at the cottonwool snowflakes falling in ranks regular as guardsmen down the glass of his window; past the symmetrical pyramids of fruit and vegetables in Mr Leyshon's, the small, thin-skinned tangerines wrapped in silver foil, the boxes of dates from North Africa. I ran so that I did not have to think of Maldwyn.

Maldwyn had been my friend as long as I could remember. There was not a time when Maldwyn had not been around. He had great advantages as a friend. Not only could he laugh more loudly than anyone else, he was so awkward that with him the simplest exercise, just walking up the street, was hilarious chaos. And his house too, his house was big and gloriously untidy. In the basement was the workshop in which his father repaired all the machines in the neighborhood, all the lawn-mowers, the electric kettles and irons, the clocks and watches. He also repaired them in the kitchen, in the garden, in the hall, wherever he happened to be. Our fathers' ancient cars were often in his yard, waiting for him to coax their tired pistons to another paroxysm of irregular combustion.

Mr. Farraday's hands held always a bundle of incomprehensible metal parts he was patiently arranging into efficiency. He'd let us watch him tease into place the cogs and rivets of some damaged artifact, telling us in his quiet voice what he was doing. Sometimes, when we were watching Mr. Farraday, Maldwyn's two sisters, long, thin and malevolent, would come round and enrage us. Then Mr. Farraday would turn us out of doors and the sisters would giggle away to play the piano in another room. Maldwyn could roar like a bull. When he did this, his sisters would put their hands to their ears and run screaming, but Mr. Farraday just smiled gently.

Maldwyn's parents had come from a village many miles away, in the west of Wales. Their house was often full of cousins from this village, smiling, talking in their open country voices. They drank a lot of tea, these cousins, and then they all went off to visit Enoch Quinell. Everybody knew Enoch Quinell, because he was a policeman and enormously fat. My father said Enoch weighed more than two hundred and eighty pounds. But Maldwyn's family knew Enoch particularly well because he, too, had come from their village and always went back there for his holidays.

We knew a lot of jokes about Enoch, about how he'd cracked the weigh bridge where the coal trucks were weighed, how he was supposed to have broken both ankles trying to stand on tip-toe. I used to think they were pretty funny jokes, but Maldwyn would be very angry if he heard one of them and offer to fight the boy who said it. He was a hopeless fighter, anybody could have picked him off with one hand, but we all liked him. On Saturday mornings he went shopping for Enoch, for food, for shaving soap, cigarettes, things like that. Sometimes I went with him.

Enoch lived in rooms above the police station, and we'd climb there, past the fire engine on the ground floor, its brass glittering, its hoses white and spotless, past the billiard room, then up the stairs to Enoch's place. Once I saw Enoch eat. He cooked for himself a steak so huge that I could find no way to describe it to my mother. And then he covered it in fried onions. Maldwyn used to get sixpence for doing Enoch's shopping.

He had been working for Enoch on Christmas Eve. I hadn't known that. All afternoon I'd been searching for him, around the back of the garages where we had a den, in the market; I couldn't find him anywhere. Just as I thought of going home, I saw Maldwyn at the top of the street. He was singing, but when I called him he stopped and waved. The lights were coming on in the houses and shops. Some children were singing carols outside Benny Everson's door. I could have told them it was a waste of time.

"Look what Enoch gave me," Maldwyn said. Enoch had given him ten shillings. We had never known such wealth.

"What are you going to do with it?" I asked, touching the silver with an envious finger.

"I'm going to buy Enoch a cigar," he said, "for Christmas. Coming over?"

We walked towards the High Street. Mr. Turner, the tobacconist, was a tall, pale man, exquisitely dressed. He had a silver snuffbox and was immaculately polite to everyone who entered his shop. I knew that he and Maldwyn would be hours choosing a cigar for Enoch. I could already hear Mr. Turner asking Maldwyn's opinion.

"Perhaps something Cuban?" Mr. Turner would say. "No? Something a little smaller, perhaps, a little milder?"

"Ugh?" Maldwyn would say, smiling, not understanding any of it, enjoying it all.

I couldn't stand it. When we got to the Market I told Maldwyn that I'd wait for him there. I told him I'd wait outside Marlow's where I could look at the brilliant windows of the sporting world, the rows of fishing rods and the racks of guns,the beautiful feathery hooks of salmon-flies in their perspex boxes, the soccer balls, the marvellous boxing shorts, glittering and colored like the peacock, the blood-red boxing gloves. Each week I spent hours at these windows and I was a long time there on Christmas Eve. Maldwyn didn't come back. At last I went home. My mother was crying and everybody in our house was quiet. Then they told me that Maldwyn was dead. He had rushed out of Mr. Turner's shop, carrying in his hand two cigars in a paper bag, and run straight under a truck.

"I've been watching for him," I said. "Outside Marlow's. He went to buy a cigar for Enoch."

I went early to bed and slept well. It didn't feel as if Maldwyn was dead. I thought of him as if he were in his house a few doors down the street, but when I walked past on Christmas morning the blinds were drawn across all the Farraday's windows and in some of the other houses too. The whole street was silent. And all that day I was lost, alone. We didn't enjoy Christmas in our house. The next day Mr. Farraday came over to say that they were going to bury Maldwyn in their village, taking him away to the little church where his grandparents were buried. He asked me to walk with the funeral to the edge of town, with five other boys.

"You were his best friend," Mr. Farraday said.

Mr. Farraday looked exactly the same as he always did, his face pink and clean, his bony hands slow. I told him that I'd like to walk in Maldwyn's funeral. I had never been to a funeral.

The day they took Maldwyn away was cold. When I got up a hard frost covered the ground and the sky was gray. At ten o'clock I went down to Maldwyn's. The other boys were already there, standing around: Danny Simpson, Urias Ward, Reggie Evans, Georgie and Bobby Rowlands. We wore our best suits, our overcoats, our scarves, our gleaming shoes. The hearse and the black cars were waiting at the curb and little knots of men stood along the pavement, talking quietly. In a little while Maldwyn's door opened and three tall men carried out the coffin. I was astonished by its length; it looked long enough to hold a man, yet Maldwyn was shorter than I. He was younger too. I hadn't expected that there would be any noise, but there was. Gentle though the bearers were, the coffin bumped softly, with blunt wooden sounds, and grated when they slid it along the chromium tracks inside the hearse. I knew that little Georgie Rowlands was scared. His eyes were pale and large and he couldn't look away. The wreaths were carried from the house and placed in a careful pile on the coffin and inside the hearse. I could see mine, made of early daffodils and other flowers I couldn't name. My card was wired to it. I had written on it, "Goodbye Maldwyn, from all at Number 24."

"You boys will march at the side of the hearse," said Mr.
Jewell, the undertaker, "three on each side, you understand?"

We nodded.

"And no playing about," Mr. Jewell said. "Just walk firmly
along. And when we get to the park gates we'll stop for a second so that you can all get safely to the side of the road. We
don't want accidents. Be careful, remember that."

"Yes," Reggie Evans said.

Danny Simpson and Georgie Rowlands were on my side
of the hearse. As we walked up the street I could see my mother
and brother, but I didn't even nod to them. They were with
a gathering of other neighbors, all looking cold and sad. We
turned and marched towards the edge of town, perhaps a mile
away. The wind, gusting and hard, blew at our legs and the
edges of our coats. There were few people to see us go. At
the park gates the whole procession stopped and we stood in
a line at the side of the road. We saw the car in which Mr. and
Mrs. Farraday sat, with their daughters. I didn't recognize them
in their unaccustomed black, but Urias Ward did. I saw Enoch
Quinell in one of the following cars, and he saw me. He looked
me full in the face and he was completely unsmiling and serious. Picking up speed, the hearse and the other cars sped up
the road, over the river bridge, out of sight. Left without a purpose, we waited until we knew they were far away.

"Let's go home through the park," Danny Simpson said.

We walked in single file along the stone parapet of the lake,
looking at the grey water. The wind, blowing without hin-
drance over its surface, had cut it into choppy waves, restless,
without pattern. Everything was cold. Out in the middle, riding the water as indifferently as if it had been a smooth summer day, were the two mute swans which lived there all year
round. They were indescribably sad and beautiful, like swans
out of some cruel story from the far north, like birds in some
cold elegy I had but dimly heard and understood only its sorrow. I remembered that these swans were said to sing only
as they died, and I resented then their patient mastery of the
water, their manifest living. And then there came unbidden into
my mind the images of all the death I knew. I saw my grandfather in his bed, when I had been taken to see him, but that

was all right because his nose was high and sharp and his teeth were too big and he hadn't looked like my grandfather. He hadn't looked like a person at all. I saw again the dead puppy I had found on the river bank, his skin peeling smoothly away from his poor flesh, and this was frightening, for he came often to terrify me in nightmares, and I also wept in pity for him when I was sick or tired. And I saw the dead butterfly I had found behind the bookshelves where it had hidden from the approach of winter. It had been a Red Admiral, my favorite butterfly, and it had died there, spread so that I could marvel at the red and white markings on its dusky wings, their powder still undisturbed. I held it on the palm of my hand and it was dry and light, so light that when I closed my eyes I could not tell that I held it, as light as dust. And thinking of the unbroken butterfly, I knew that I would never again see Maldwyn Farraday, nor hear his voice, nor wake in the morning to the certainty that we would spend the day together. He was gone forever. A great and painful emptiness was in my chest and my throat. I stopped walking and took from my overcoat pocket the last of my Christmas chocolate, a half-pound block. I called the boys around me and, breaking the chocolate into sections, I divided it among us. There were two sections over, and I gave them to little Georgie Rowlands because he was the youngest. Tears were pouring down Reggie Evans' cheeks and the wind blew them across his nose and onto the collar of his overcoat.

"It's the wind," he said. "The bloody wind makes your eyes water."

He could scarcely speak and we stood near him, patting his shoulders, our mouths filled with chocolate, saying yes yes, the wind, the cold wind. But we were all crying, we were all bitterly weeping, our cheeks were wet and stinging with the harsh salt of our tears, we were overwhelmed by the recognition of our unique and common knowledge, and we had nowhere to turn for comfort but to ourselves.

Some Opposites
of Good

When Mark opened the front door he could see Useless Lewis waiting for him at the corner of the street. Useless was poised in a tense crouch, his face tight and snarling. Without mercy he gunned down Mr. Sweet's black cat, pumping bullets into its rich fur as it sat sunning itself in the doorway of the shop; then, straightening, he sprayed the street with bullets, smiling grimly at the patterned dust he raised.

"Goodbye, Mark," called Mark's mother from her kitchen.

Useless sweetly holstered the clenched fists of his imagined six-shooters, caught invisible reins in the tips of his fingers, and cantered down the road, slapping his haunches with the flat of his hand, whinnying. Useless was being the world's greatest cowboy.

"Hi," he said to Mark.

On the way to school nothing escaped the vigilance of Useless' accurate fingers. He shot the tops from bottles of milk as they stood in doorways, he blasted passing cyclists as they sped innocently to work, he exploded the wheels of cars. At street corners he stood six feet tall, surveying the scene with his bleak, sardonic eye before calling Mark forward to walk in safety among the traps and ambushes laid in the shadows of the morning streets. Useless shot his way through them all.

He was Mark's best friend, but he was an awful nuisance. Mark was glad when they got to school.

Although it was early, Jack Mathias would certainly be there before them. Jack Mathias lived a long way off, in a cottage on the mountain, and his mother was dead. When Mr. Mathias went to work, very early, Jack would have to leave too, because his father would lock the house. Jack would have to wait alone in the school yard until someone came along to talk to him. He had dirty teeth and his shirts were always crumpled and dirty because of his mother, but everybody liked him. He was fifteen years old, a big boy and a great footballer, the best in school. He was teaching Mark to play.

They played in the open shed that ran down one side of the yard, where the boys sheltered when it was raining. It was paved with granite slabs, a yard square, made smooth and polished by the running boots of generations of boys. Jack Mathias was waiting there, in the shade of the roof. Between his feet he had the little flat stone they used instead of a ball and he was flicking it gently this way and that, absorbed in the performance of his faultless skill.

Useless was already stalking up the yard, stiff-legged and menacing, ready to shoot it out with any black evil, the thunder of his avenging guns held silent under his thumbs.

"Keck! Keck!" he said, bringing down two passing crows.

Mark ran into the shed.

"Right," said Jack Mathias, "you get five goals start, OK?"

They ran until the shed was so full of boys they could no longer play without interruption, and then Jack Mathias showed Mark how to swerve and how to push the ball around one side of an opponent and run around the other.

"You'll have to learn to use your left foot," said Jack Mathias. "Watch this."

He collected the stone with a cool sweep of his leg and, in the same movement, pushed it in front of him. But even as he jumped into his first stride, his right knee raised, the whole world stopped. Jack Mathias hung, arrested in midflight, long arms aloft. The little stone went bobbling on, scuttling over the flagstones, making a tiny hollow noise, the only moving thing in the school yard. Everywhere groups of boys held their

72

frozen attitudes, older boys like careless and lounging statues, small boys balancing precariously at the edges of energy. The first whistle had gone, and nobody must move. Mark, without the stir of a visible muscle, got ready for the second whistle. When it came, he shot into action, racing for the class lines in front of the school building. But he was a long way off and had to find a place near the end of the queue. Useless was four or five boys in front of him, and Mark waved to him. But Useless didn't see him. Useless had gone to live inside his head, he was galloping the wide and sunlit prairies of his imagination.

The teacher on duty was Witty Thomas, small, plump and beautifully dressed. This morning he wore a suit of silver-gray and his shirt was a rich cream color. His tie was red with little silver flowers woven in it, and the fresh rose in his buttonhole was as yellow as sunshine. He bounced about in front of the files of boys, his face pink, sending his thin voice shouting into the air, waving his arms at the sauntering impertinence of the older boys as they came slowly into a reluctant line.

"Come, come on!" screamed Mr. Thomas. "Do you think you've got all day?"

The big boys idled along, some smiling openly at histrionic Mr. Thomas, some, their heads turned away, ignoring him.

Witty, in an impotent fury, danced toward them on his little glittering shoes, and, as he came near, Useless, concentrating, steadying his aim with the coldest deliberation, shot away, one after the other, the pearl buttons on Mr. Thomas' vest. He was narrowing his eyes to focus on the last button when Mr. Thomas saw him.

"What's this?" cried Witty Thomas, suddenly and terrifyingly jovial. "And what is this? Would you like to shoot me, Lewis?"

He grabbed Useless by the collar and pulled him out, shaking him and jerking him. Mark could see the nailed soles of Useless' boots as his legs swung in the air.

A small, delighted cheer came from the boys, but Mr. Thomas ignored it. He just smiled his frightening smile and began to cuff Useless' head.

"So you'd like to shoot me, eh, Lewis?" Witty Thomas said. "But you wouldn't dare, would you, would you, would you!"

He punctuated his speech with quick slaps, but Useless cleverly burrowed close to him, burying his head against Mr. Thomas' round little stomach so that the man couldn't swing at him.

"Leave him alone," shouted Jack Mathias in his laughing, man's voice. "Pick someone your own size! Go it little 'un!'"

Everybody knew that Mr. Thomas was afraid to touch Jack Mathias, because Jack's father was so big and rough.

Useless came back to his place and he was smiling all over. He wasn't frightened, Mark could see that.

"Fifty years old," said Damion Davies, who was tall and thin and lazy. "Fifty years old and still heavyweight champion. Just fancy!"

"Shut it, Davies," said Mr. Thomas, panting, "or you'll get the same."

"Such a temper, too," said Damion in his languid voice, and he rolled his eyes in mock admiration.

"Lead on!" cried Mr. Thomas, pointing, as if he were leading an expedition into wildest Tibet. "Lead on, the first row!"

Useless and Mark bent their knees and slid into the cold, stiff hinged desk they shared, being careful of the splinters, sharp as frost, that would run into their thighs. They took out their books and placed them neatly, ready for work. Mark looked at his friend. The marks of Mr. Thomas' grabbing fingers were plain on the back of Useless' neck and his right ear was blazing red. You could almost warm your hands against it.

"Does it hurt?" Mark whispered.

"Of course not," said Useless, "Witty couldn't hurt a fly."

Useless couldn't read. Each morning Mark would have to help him, listening to him mutter aloud the separate, clumsy words as he stumbled from sentence to sentence. Mark worked hard with Useless. He had stood for hours outside shops, making Useless read the price cards and the advertisements for chocolates, but it was no use. It was as if words had no meaning for Useless. He could not see that they added to each other as you said them, that the sum of the words was interesting and surprising. He listened to Useless drop the flat sounds one by one out of his mouth.

"Don't forget," said Useless between sentences. "It's Friday, pass it on."

Most Friday mornings Mr. Treharne, the headmaster, came in to test the boys in spelling, in mental arithmetic and in the plurals and opposites of words. Mark enjoyed this. He would sit upright in his desk, his arms folded in front of him, hoping Mr. Treharne would ask him some spectacularly difficult question. When this happened Mark's mind would become as clear as glass and he would see the answer right in the center of his thinking. But very often Mr. Treharne didn't ask him anything at all, preferring to spend his time being angry at those poor boys who couldn't answer anything. Useless was one of these.

It was strange about Useless. He was brave, he was loyal, he knew a lot of jokes. When he pretended, you could believe in the unseen world Useless would make around him. Mark just knew, just from watching Useless, that he had ridden a white horse to school that morning, you could see it. Although your real eyes would still see only a boy with short hair and freckles on his neck. Useless knew about real horses, too. His father had a pony and cart and one Sunday in the summer the boys had gone to a field near the river and caught the pony. Useless had held an apple in his hand and the pony had eaten it, very gently, with his crude brown teeth. Then Useless had leapt cleverly on the animal's back, wrapping the coarse hair of its mane in his fists. He'd hung on for a long while as the pony galloped clumsily around the field. A horse was unexpectedly heavy. Mark could remember the surprising weight of its hooves when they pounded the earth like an immense drum. In the end Useless had fallen off and lay on his back, puffing and laughing. He hoped Useless would be able to answer some of Mr. Treharne's questions. He looked over at Useless and his ear was pretty nearly the normal color.

Mr. Pascoe, their own teacher, put his hand gently on Mark's shoulder, reminding him to get on with his work. The boy bent his head over his book and began to write. Mr. Pascoe was young and kind and this was his very first job. All the boys liked him. As he wrote, Mark still thought of Useless, fallen and laughing in the grass by the river, remembering too the dark green of the clover patches, and their pink flowers. Mark began to write a story of two friends who had gone to a summer field and found there a horse so gentle, its breath so fragrant of sweet clover, so amenable and intelligent an animal that it was more companion than beast. It was thin, and seemed to have been cruelly treated, but there was about it a recognizable air of breeding, of a royal pride. For weeks, in the story, the two boys had coveted the horse, exulting in its increasing strength and beauty. Mark began to describe the glowing perfection of his coat, its docile manner, its unassuming pride. There was no doubt, Mark felt, that here he was making a prince among horses, a true Arabian. He was about to send all three of his heroes on some epic journey when the headmaster walked in.

Mark slowly put away his story. He would have liked to have returned his lovely pony to its true owner, an eagle-profiled sheikh who lived in a camp high in the Atlas Mountains. After years of adventure, the boys would have handed over the superb horse. They would have been rewarded with jewels, made members of this most savage of Bedouin tribes. A great feast would have been made in their honor, with kebabs and raw sheep's eyes. They would have flown home famous and wealthy.

"Hurry up, boy," said Mr. Treharne, tapping Mark's desk with his cane.

Mr. Treharne was not big, but he walked with compensating dignity and importance. He carried with him his own silence, hard and painful, and it was this sensation that filled the room now, as cold water might fill a bowl. Mr. Treharne put his cane under his arm and drew back his lips in a grimace, revealing white teeth regular and artificial as a doll's.

Mr. Pascoe stood nervously near his high desk.

"Sit down, Pascoe," said Mr. Treharne. "Sit down, man. Where's your chalk?"

He took some chalk from the table and stood before the boys. The air in the room was so still that Mark thought he could have plucked it like a guitar string. Then the testing began.

It was not too bad. First they did some multiplication tables and then questions about buying and selling things, buns, postage stamps, gallons of milk. Mr. Treharne spoke very slowly and clearly, making sure every boy had heard; and then he'd pounce, his rigid cane pointed at arm's length, on some unready boy. He knew exactly which poor boys would find the questions impossible to answer. But most of them were prepared and alert, answering Mr. Treharne confidently. It was going to be a happy morning. Even Mr. Treharne was nearly smiling.

He turned about slowly, looking meditatively from one boy's face to another, but Mark wasn't fooled. He knew better than to relax.

"Galaxy," Mr. Treharne snapped, his stick under Mark's nose. "You boy, spell galaxy."

That was an easy one.

"You're a sharp lad," said Mr. Treharne, "a bright lad."

He leaned away as if to ask some other boy a word, and then whipped back.

"Idiosyncrasy," he said.

Flawlessly and successively Mark spelled idiosyncrasy, brontosaurus, yacht, zephyr, seraph, commission.

Mark was elated. It was like playing some vitally skillful and dangerous game, in which Mr. Treharne was attacking him with something as sharp and violent as a sword, and only by the most agile and determined techniques could Mark beat him away. When the headmaster asked him no more words Mark knew he had won. He felt hard and shining, as if every bit of him was clean and smooth, working with a silent perfection. He imagined all the world's words waiting for him to order them into formal and meticulous patterns. He sat upright on his bench, his back achingly straight, triumphant. It was a little time before he could listen to what was happening in the room.

Mr. Treharne was no longer pleased. David Sheppard and Ronnie Howells were standing up, their hands behind their backs, unable to give the opposite of sour, and Mr. Treharne was clicking his tongue in irritation. Two little red spots appeared on his cheekbones. Mark looked about; nobody appeared to know. He put up his hand.

"Put down your hand, Watkins," snarled Mr. Treharne, not looking at him. "You've had your moment of splendor. Are you idiot enough to think that you alone know the opposite of sour?"

Mark pulled his hand down. Somebody tittered.

"The next boy to laugh," said Mr. Treharne, "will find I have a painful cure for that condition. It is no matter for amusement to find we have two ignorant and lazy boys in a class."

His face was sullen, the corners of his mouth drawn sternly down.

"The opposite of sour is sweet," he said. "Sweet. Do you hear me, Howells, Sheppard? Sit down. I have no patience with you."

He watched the two boys sit. There was not a sound in the room, not even a breath. Little Frankie Rossi, the smallest boy in the class, stared terrified in front of him. Then he began, very slightly, to tremble.

Cautiously the boys waited, careful to do nothing that would disturb the man's dry temper, inflammable as straw.

"There will be others," said Mr. Treharne, "other boys, lazy fellows all of them, who will not be able to answer the simplest of questions!"

The boys shivered as he looked at them.

"Rossi, for example," shouted Mr. Treharne.

It was not fair to pick on Frankie Rossi. Although he was small, he was always cheerful and smiling. He and Useless were the worst readers in the class.

"Rossi," said Mr. Treharne, "give us the benefit of your erudition. Give us the opposites of long, dry, little, thin, good."

He spat out each word, his face red and angry, cracking the face of the table with his cane, each stroke leaving a clean brown mark in the film of chalk dust on the surface.

Frankie Rossi began to cry, softly and quietly. Mr. Pascoe was standing behind the headmaster, his face pale, perfectly still except for his hands. His fingers were lifting and falling against the cloth of his jacket. There was no other movement.

Then Mr. Treharne was striding between the desks, asking boy after boy for opposites to those simple words. It was as if a great storm, an unimaginable violence, had entered the familiar room and ripped away its safety. Mr. Treharne moved and spoke with such fury that nobody had time to answer him.

At last he stopped, so close to Mark that the boy could feel his nearness. Mr. Treharne was looking at Useless.

"And now we come to Lewis," said Mr. Treharne, almost whispering.

Useless stood in his desk, his legs bent where the bench pressed against the back of his knees. The whole desk was shaking slightly, as if it was alive.

"Lewis," said Mr. Treharne, "I want you to tell me the opposite of good. Tell us all, Lewis, we shall await your answer."

Mark let out his breath in relief. He had been praying as intensely as he knew how, willing Mr. Treharne to ask Useless something easy. Now everything would be all right.

But Useless did not answer.

"Think hard, Lewis," said Mr. Treharne. "Think hard. It will be the cane if you do not give me the correct answer."

Mark could see Useless' legs quivering, he could almost smell his fear. In an agony, Mark urged his friend to speak, sending the silent words across to him.

Useless lifted his head.

"Rotten, sir," he blurted.

The brilliance and unexpectedness of Useless' word were like the sunshine, lighting up Mark's mind. He turned in astonishment to his friend, almost clapping aloud.

"Keep still, Watkins," Mr. Treharne said to him.

He whipped his cane through the air, making a pliant and cruel whistling.

"Come out, Lewis," he said.

Mr. Treharne could not have heard Useless. Mark put up his hand to explain.

"Put down your hand," shouted Mr. Treharne, in a sudden explosion of renewed temper, "I shan't tell you again."

But Mark knew there was a mistake. He smiled up at Mr. Treharne.

"But sir," he said, "Useless' father, sir, he keeps a fruit shop, and he sells the good apples, sir, and he throws away the rotten . . ."

"Come out, Watkins," said Mr. Treharne.

Mark scrambled out of his desk and stood beside Useless. "Hold out your hand," Mr. Treharne said to Useless.

Mark could not think that it was happening, that Mr. Treharne could have failed to understand the wonderful accuracy of Useless' word. He was confused and indignant.

"Sir," he said, "you mustn't cane him. Rotten is a good opposite!"

And suddenly Mr. Treharne was before him, grabbing Mark's wrist with terrifying ferocity, pulling the boy's arm out straight before him. He rapped Mark's knuckles sharply with the cane to open the hand. Then he raised the stick above his head and brought it cutting down on the small flesh in a full arc, across the base of the palm and the soft fingers. At first there was no pain at all, for a slight moment only, and then an agony so far beyond anything he had experienced before took away the boy's breath and left him gasping. He could not see anything and was only dimly aware that at his side Useless was being punished in his turn. Mr. Treharne bundled the shocked boys into their seats. Mark held his burning hand between his knees and put his head on the hard wood of the desk so that nobody could see his weeping face.

After Mr. Treharne had left the room, Mr. Pascoe came over to Mark, talking quietly to him, trying to help him. The bell rang for morning break and Mr. Pascoe let Mark stay in the room and Useless stayed with him.

"The pain'll go after a bit," Useless said.

But all through the morning, long after he was able to look objectively at his beaten hand and touch the swollen skin of his fingers, the boy would shake with occasional sobs. He mourned not so much for his vanishing pain, nor the indignity of his beating, but because his safe world had collapsed about him. He wept because he had been shown a world without hope and without justice, a world in which the very words were without meaning.

In the West
Country

When I was a young man, I taught at a school in Yeovil, a small town in Somerset. Nothing much happened in Yeovil. Each morning my children came dreamily to school, their fathers worked in shops or dairies or breweries, their mothers made the gloves for which the town had a reputation. Oh, I liked Yeovil very much. Its citizens spoke slowly, with a soft, creamy accent; its houses were built of golden, local stone—the gentle Ham stone; its life was slow and comfortable; I had many friends there. There was nothing wrong with the town, yet I never stayed there a day longer than was necessary. The last hours of every term would find me with my bags packed, waiting for the bell that would end school and set me striding away for Pen Mill Station, a few hundred yards down the road, on the edge of town. I always went home to Wales and I always went by train.

Nothing would be moving at Pen Mill Station. Only rarely would there be someone at the barrier to examine my ticket. Once inside, I could sometimes see, far away down the platform, a lone porter sitting on a trolley, looking steadfastly into the distance, not even reading. There would never be a train. But eventually one would arrive—a small, meandering train with an air of having strayed in from earlier, more rustic times; and when, at last, it set off again it did nothing to dispel this impression. There probably was a village in Somerset at which

81

it did not stop but I cannot remember one. On we went, our roundabout, leisurely journey interrupted at such conurbations as Marston Magna, Queen Camel, Sparkford, Castle Cary, Bruton, Frome, Westbury.

It was at Westbury, on a day when we travelled more haltingly than usual, that I once left the train. It was Sunday, a day of clear summer, the air dry and cloudless, little motes of sun haze dancing in the yellow light. I walked out of the station and found, at the end of a green lane, a lake, like a mirage, fringed by reeds. There, on that lake, I saw for the first time the great crested grebe, a diving bird I had only read about. It swam low in the water, its dark body almost lost, its long neck holding aloft its ruffed and regal head; and it was joined by another grebe, and then one more, and yet another, until there were six of these remarkable birds swimming, or vanishing into the water. If it was water. It was an element so rare and fine, so unruffled by any passage of air of bird, that the very reflections of those grebes floated beneath their bodies complete in feather, in color, in action. Waterdrops fell down from each flawless bird and up from each immaculate image, dissolving in each other as they met, in an equal harmony. I forgot the train, but when, hot, dusty, and amazed, I got back to the station, it was still there, somnolent and good-tempered, waiting for me.

On the other hand, if my friend Barney Eagleton was driving, we sometimes made very good time, rattling through those delicious fields as if there were in life a real purpose, a sense of urgent destiny. But this was a deception. Barney was also an enthusiastic bird-watcher, and a specialist at that—a heron specialist. I think Barney knew more about herons than any other man alive. Somewhere in north Somerset our train ran along a high embankment for a distance of several hundred yards. We could look down from our carriage windows on the tops of great elms in whose wide branches herons had for generations nested. In late spring, after the young birds had hatched, any engine driven by Barney Eagleton would rumble past these nests with infinite, heavy caution. And then it would stop. People would pull down their windows and lean

out, watching the young birds wave their snakelike heads, nodding approval to Barney as he stood in his cab owning the
whole flock. A few impatient souls—lovers, perhaps, or men
from Bristol—would begin to mutter and look at their watches;
and at last, bored beyond watching by the repetitive and
unimaginative behavior of young herons, we all would yell
insults or instructions at Barney. He would sigh, turn to his
levers, and, later than ever, we would roll ponderously away.

This was near Bradford-on-Avon, as we entered the valley
of the Avon. Now a perceptible change would come over our
progress, whether Barney drove us or not. We were nearing
civilization; the great cities were coming toward us. Our speed
became smarter, we were signalled away from the little sta-
tions with an urban confidence and panache. We left behind
the huge tithe barn of Bradford-on-Avon and the weir below
which the river holds great pike. Quite soon we would reach
Bath.

Such cities are not best approached by train. They were
there—expansive, prosperous, established—long before
Trevithick drove his long-stacked old steam engine, the first
in the world to roll on its own wheels under its own power,
down the valley in Wales where I was born. The railway tends
to enter old cities apologetically, running behind the backs of
unimportant houses, hidden behind tall walls at the perimeter
of things. And Bath is a great European city, important even
before the Romans rebuilt it. Our train, it is true, made the best
of things outside of town, steaming along the valley with an
impressive directness. But soon enough—as soon as we left
Bathampton station—the very weight and presence of the city
forced us in a wide curve to the south. Not much of the famous
crescents and terraces could be seen from our windows. We
would sidle into Bath Spa Station, clamped in an elbow of the
river between Dorchester Street and Claverton Street, and then
we'd set off for Bristol—a brief run. And after that we'd rattle
through the long tunnel beneath the Bristol Channel and come
up among the hills and quick vowels of Wales. On the last possible day I would do the whole journey in reverse, ending in
darkness among the little fields and lit farms of Somerset,
leaving Pen Mill Station still harmlessly deserted, walking the

evening streets in the bland Somerset air. Bath was unimportant to me, a back cloth, an incident in a journey.

Yet years later I went to teach in Bath. It was something I never got used to. I lived in a flat in the city, and every evening I would go to sleep knowing that on the floors above my head other men were already sleeping, or preparing to sleep. We lived in layers, and this was foreign to me. Always I felt about me the whispers and rustling of other lives; I was aware of the great, serious eyes of people not known to me as they turned by night to their partners and began to speak of the little deaths of their hours. The tall house was full of night-long sibilance. In hot weather I kept my windows open and listened to the one tree in the yard gasping. I cannot say I liked living there.

But there was much that was delightful. Each evening after work, and at weekends, I walked the streets of Bath—Broad Street and Green Street, Lilliput Lane and Orange Grove, Miller Street and Great Pulteney Street. Sometimes I went along the riverbank, with anglers stationed every yard of the way, up to Pulteney Bridge, and higher. I travelled to the villages which lie snugly about in the combs and hollows of the round hills: Monkton Farleigh and Monkton Combe, Limpley Stoke, Wellow, Englishcombe, Newton St. Loe, Swainswick. Best of all I liked wet nights when the streets were empty. Once, on a night of appalling and splendid downpour, I alone saw a screech owl perched on the roof of the Guildhall, in the heart of the city. He cried aloud at the flattening rain, and I, sheltering momentarily in the post-office doorway to see him better, saluted him, knowing him to be, like me, an invader from simpler places. In the summer I sat on Beechen Cliff and watched the city below my feet. The city began to haunt me.

More and more, in the mists that hung, imperceptibly frail and shifting, at the corners of early morning streets and above the hedges in the parks, I began to see Bath as it really was—made for people long dead. The parks and crescents presented themselves to me as if they were the calm watercolors of the eighteenth century. Autumn began to thin the streets. I would sniff the air outside the Assembly Rooms, certain I could detect the pungent ghost of a vanished snuff, blown away long ago by two centuries of weather, its lost, rich smell an aroma of the memory only. The world drove steadily into winter. In the evening, as I walked over Pulteney Bridge in the crisp dark, it seemed to me that we, the living, were the ghosts, we the haunting shadows, that the city existed in all its truth and formal grace for older lives than ours. A week before Christmas a muffling snow fell in the night and silenced everything.

That morning I went into Victoria Gardens. It was Saturday, normally the busiest of days, but only a few shopping women braved the streets, on necessary errands, and one or two children stamped knee-deep in the snow. It was bitterly cold, sly winds whipping from the curved surfaces of the snow a stinging powder, driving it against the wrists, against the cold cheeks and the neck. The park was deserted, apart from a black Labrador, thickset and sturdy against the whiteness, stumping along some way off. I walked under the chestnuts aimlessly, head down against the gusts.

"Hey, Doc," cried a voice. "Hey, Doctor!"

A big man was sitting on one of the park benches. He had cleared it of snow, and he sat there, expansive and relaxed, one arm extended along the back, as comfortable as if it were summer. He sat there unmoving in the gray light, his face under the shadow of a wide-brimmed hat, a scarf knotted at his throat.

"Doc," he called. "Hey, come on over!"

Even close up I could not see his face clearly, but he was a remarkable man; his size alone made him that. He sat on the park bench as I might a footstool. A thin raincoat was pulled across his great body, one hand, as large and white as a plate, rested calmly on his knee.

"How you keeping, Doc?" he said. "This weather trouble you?"

"No," I said. "I seem to manage."

"You always was one for keeping warm," the man said, and chuckled. "You always was," he said again.

I looked about me. The lawns were hidden under snow blown by the inconstant wind, the trees at the edge of the park were insubstantial as smoke, the dog had disappeared. The big man and I were alone. I had never seen him before.

"Oh, you always could look after yourself," he said. "When you was in the navy, I told your father: don't worry about him, I said, he'll not go short. He can look after himself."

I had nothing to say. I stood in front of the huge man as he sat on his bench near the restless bushes. He was quite old, I thought. His feet, in worn black oxfords, were enormous. I have never been in the navy.

Suddenly he took his arm from the back of the bench and bent forward. I could see the top of his worn hat. There was a black patch of grease at the crown.

"Here, Doc," he said, "have a look at this."

He rolled up the right leg of this trousers. His leg was bandaged from ankle to knee, the bandage itself frayed and stained.

"Do you think this right," he said his voice indistinct as he bent down unwrapping the bandage, "that my leg should be in this state? All these years, in a state like this?"

He lifted his great head and I could look full in his upturned face. He had been very handsome and was still impressive—a face clear-featured and aristocratic, sensitive, the nostrils high and beautifully formed, the mouth clean-lipped and firm. But his eyes were innocent and troubled, like a child's eyes, like the eyes of a child who suddenly does not understand the world.

"I was in the navy, Doctor," he said. "Over twenty years, I was a matelot. You know I was; you saw me. Do you think I ought to have a leg like this?"

He rubbed his sleeve across his face. His mouth began to tremble.

"Let's see it," I said.

He straightened the leg in front of me. The flesh was covered with running ulcers, some as big as a pinhead, some the size of a man's palm. The whole world seemed to have shrunk to a few square yards, a small, cold space just large enough to hold the old man and me. He was looking at me with an unnerving intensity of trust.

"It's bad," I said. "Quite bad."

"What shall I do, Doc?" he said.

"Keep it warm and clean," I said. "Eat as well as you can, get up to the hospital and ask for treatment. Go there as soon as you can make it."

"I will," said the big man. "I'll go today."

"Wrap it up now," I said. "Don't let the cold get at it."

"Somehow it's easier in the cold weather," he said, bending down obediently and winding the narrow cotton around his shin. "The hot weather plays havoc with it."

There was no reason I should have said any of this to the old man. The unreality of the situation, the feeling that the park itself was taken from the known world and floating into limbo, the dim light and the misty edges of the trees, the bitter cold which made thinking slow and inaccurate—all contrived to make me accept a different identity, the one recognized by the old man. I turned away and walked down the path. After a few yards I stopped. I wanted to tell him to make sure to get to the hospital, that he must demand treatment. I turned around, but he wasn't there.

I ran back to the bench. It was still clear of snow, although a few large flakes settled on it as I stood there. I could see where I had stood in front of the old man, I could fit my shoes exactly into the deep, deep holes I had made, and I thought I could see the enormous hollows from the old man's feet.

I hurried into Royal Crescent and along Brock Street. I had never been so cold. Over the circus the heavy sky held a few threads of ominous yellow light. Before I reached home the snow began in earnest again.

That afternoon I had a letter inviting me to accept a teaching job in Middlesex—a job I'd always wanted and never thought I'd have. It meant immediate preparation. I telephoned a reply and began at once to put my affairs in order, to leave the West Country. I saw my landlord, paid my rent, said goodbye to some people I knew. I didn't own much—a few books, some clothes, a packet of letters. On Thursday the snow had all gone, although the weather was still unfriendly. I walked over to Victoria Gardens and went right through, from one gate to the other, but here was no sign of the big man. The next day I walked down the hill toward the station, and bought a paper at the kiosk, and waited for my train. I was ready to go. I can remember now how eager I was to be gone. I walked up and down, tensely, lightly, like a sprinter before moving to his blocks. A fussy little engine came in on the opposite track, a few nondescript country coaches behind it. The driver leaned from his cab and shouted to me. He was red-faced, slow of speech, smiling. Barney Eagleton. He looked wonderful.

"How you been, then?" he called, his voice rich as cream.

His peaked cap, shining with oil, was perched comfortably on his head. He leaned his forearms on the edge of his cab.

"Barney, you old dog, it's good to see you."

We grinned at each other across the width of the track.

"How's the herons?" I shouted.

He stopped smiling. "They chopped down them elms up the line," he called. "A lovely heronry, that was—ever so old. Chaps as did it ought to be shot. Lovely birds, them was."

"Ever see the purple heron, Barney?" I asked him. "Lives in Spain and Greece and France and northern Italy?"

"No," he said. "It's just the plain old heron I see."

"Or the great white heron or the squacco heron or the blue heron from North America?"

"Ah, don't," said Barney. "You'll drive me crazy."

"Or the little egret or the buffbacked heron or the little bittern—great birds all?"

"What birds," said Barney, "what marvelous birds!"

I was so pleased to see old Barney that delight made me eloquent. "The night heron, Barney," I shouted, "the beautiful night heron from the Mediterranean, with its red eyes and its long drooping white crest?"

"Splendid birds," Barney raised his voice to the sky. "All fine birds, and I wish they all lived in Somerset."

I grinned across the lines at Barney.

"When you coming back to Yeovil?" he yelled.

A guard blew his whistle. Barney rolled his eyes, waved, and eased his engine out of the station.

I would never go back to Yeovil. Sooner or later all heronries fall. The train that was to take me from the West Country pulled in from Bristol—long, smooth, efficient as a bullet. *Gwlad yr haf* is what the Welsh call Somerset—the Land of Summer.

Shaving

Earlier, when Barry had left the house to go to the game, an overnight frost had still been thick on the roads, but the brisk April sun had soon dispersed it, and now he could feel the spring warmth on his back through the thick tweed of his coat. His left arm was beginning to stiffen up where he'd jarred it in a tackle, but it was nothing serious. He flexed his shoulders against the tightness of his jacket and was surprised again by the unexpected weight of his muscles, the thickening strength of his body. A few years back, he thought, he had been a small, unimportant boy, one of a swarming gang laughing and jostling to school, hardly aware that he possessed an identity. But time had transformed him. He walked solidly now, and often alone. He was tall, strongly made, his hands and feet were adult and heavy, the rooms in which all his life he'd moved had grown too small for him. Sometimes a devouring restlessness drove him from the house to walk long distances in the dark. He hardly understood how it had happened. Amused and quiet, he walked the High Street among the morning shoppers.

He saw Jackie Bevan across the road and remembered how, when they were both six years old, Jackie had swallowed a pin. The flustered teachers had clucked about Jackie as he stood there, bawling, cheeks awash with tears, his nose wet. But now Jackie was tall and suave, his thick, pale hair sleekly tailored,

89

his gray suit enviable. He was talking to a girl as golden as a daffodil. "Hey, hey!" called Jackie. "How's the athlete, how's Barry-boy?"

He waved a graceful hand at Barry.

"Come and talk to Sue," he said.

Barry shifted his bag to his left hand and walked over, forming in his mind the answers he'd make to Jackie's questions.

"Did we win?" Jackie asked. "Was the old Barry Stanford magic in glittering evidence yet once more this morning? Were the invaders sent hunched and silent back to their hovels in the hills? What was the score? Give us an epic account, Barry, without modesty or delay. This is Sue, by the way."

"I've seen you about," the girl said.

"You could hardly miss him," said Jackie. "Four men, roped together, spent a week climbing him—they thought he was Everest. He ought to carry a warning beacon, he's a danger to aircraft."

"Silly," said the girl, smiling at Jackie. "He's not much taller than you are."

She had a nice voice, too.

"We won," Barry said. "Seventeen points to three, and it was a good game. The ground was hard, though."

He could think of nothing else to say.

"Let's all go for a frivolous cup of coffee," Jackie said. "Let's celebrate your safe return from the rough fields of victory. We could pour libations all over the floor for you."

"I don't think so," Barry said. "Thanks. I'll go straight home."

"Okay," said Jackie, rocking on his heels so that the sun could shine on his smile. "How's your father?"

"No better," Barry said. "He's not going to get better."

"Yes, well," said Jackie, serious and uncomfortable, "tell him my mother and father ask about him."

"I will," Barry promised. "He'll be pleased."

Barry dropped the bag in the front hall and moved into the room which had been the dining room until his father's illness. His father lay in the white bed, his long body gaunt, his still head scarcely denting the pillow. He seemed asleep, thin blue lids covering his eyes, but when Barry turned away he spoke.

"Hello, son," he said. "Did you win?"

His voice was a dry, light rustling, hardly louder than the breath which carried it. Its sound moved Barry to a compassion that almost unmanned him, but he stepped close to the bed and looked down at the dying man.

"Yes," he said. "We won fairly easily. It was a good game."

His father lay with his eyes closed, inert, his breath irregular and shallow.

"Did you score?" he asked.

"Twice," Barry said. "I had a try in each half."

He thought of the easy certainty with which he'd caught the ball before his second try; casually, almost arrogantly he had taken it on the tips of his fingers, on his full burst for the line, breaking the fullback's tackle. Nobody could have stopped him. But watching his father's weakness he felt humble and ashamed, as if the morning's game, its urgency and effort, was not worth talking about. His father's face, fine-skinned and pallid, carried a dark stubble of beard, almost a week's growth, and his obstinate, strong hair stuck out over his brow.

"Good," said his father, after a long pause. "I'm glad it was a good game."

Barry's mother bustled about the kitchen, a tempest of orderly energy.

"Your father's not well," she said. "He's down today, feels depressed. He's a particular man, your father. He feels dirty with all that beard on him."

She slammed shut the stove door.

"Mr. Cleaver was supposed to come up and shave him," she said, "and that was three days ago. Little things have always worried your father, every detail must be perfect for him."

Barry filled a glass with milk from the refrigerator. He was very thirsty.

"I'll shave him," he said.

His mother stopped, her head on one side.

"Do you think you can?" she asked. "He'd like it if you can."

"I can do it," Barry said.

91

He washed his hands as carefully as a surgeon. His father's razor was in a blue leather case, hinged at the broad edge and with one hinge broken. Barry unfastened the clasp and took out the razor. It had not been properly cleaned after its last use and lather had stiffened into hard yellow rectangles between the teeth of the guard. There were water-shaped rust stains, brown as chocolate, on the surface of the blade. Barry removed it, throwing it in the wastebin. He washed the razor until it glistened, and dried it on a soft towel, polishing the thin handle, rubbing its metal head to a glittering shine. He took a new blade from its waxed envelope, the paper clinging to the thin metal. The blade was smooth and flexible to the touch, the little angles of its cutting clearly defined. Barry slotted it into the grip of the razor, making it snug and tight in the head.

The shaving soap, hard, white, richly aromatic, was kept in a wooden bowl. Its scent was immediately evocative and Barry could almost see his father in the days of his health, standing before his mirror, thick white lather on his face and neck. As a little boy Barry had loved the generous perfume of the soap, had waited for his father to lift the razor to his face, for one careful stroke to take away the suds in a clean revelation of the skin. Then his father would renew the lather with a few sweeps of his brush, one with an ivory handle and the bristles worn, which he still used.

His father's shaving mug was a thick cup, plain and serviceable. A gold line ran outside the rim of the cup, another inside, just below the lip. Its handle was large and sturdy, and the face of the mug carried a portrait of the young Queen Elizabeth II, circled by a wreath of leaves, oak perhaps, or laurel. A lion and unicorn balanced precariously on a scroll above her crowned head, and the Union Jack, the Royal Standard, and other flags were furled on each side of the portrait. And beneath it all, in small black letters, ran the legend: "Coronation June 2nd 1953." The cup was much older than Barry. A pattern of faint translucent cracks, fine as a web, had worked itself haphazardly, invisibly almost, through the white glaze. Inside, on the bottom, a few dark bristles were lying, loose and dry. Barry shook them out, then held the cup in his hand, feeling its solidness. Then he washed it ferociously, until it was clinically clean.

Methodically he set everything on a tray, razor, soap, brush, towels. Testing the hot water with a finger, he filled the mug and put that, too, on the tray. His care was absorbed, ritualistic. Satisfied that his preparations were complete, he went downstairs, carrying the tray with one hand.

His father was waiting for him. Barry set the tray on a bedside table and bent over his father, sliding an arm under the man's thin shoulders, lifting him without effort so that he sat against the high pillows.

"By God, you're strong," his father said. He was as breathless as if he'd been running.

"So are you," said Barry.

"I was," his father said. "I used to be strong once."

He sat exhausted against the pillows.

"We'll wait a bit," Barry said.

"You could have used your electric razor," his father said. "I expected that."

"You wouldn't like it," Barry said. "You'll get a closer shave this way."

He placed the large towel about his father's shoulders.

"Now," he said, smiling down.

The water was hot in the thick cup. Barry wet the brush and worked up the lather. Gently he built up a covering of soft foam on the man's chin, on his cheeks and his stark cheekbones.

"You're using a lot of soap," his father said.

"Not too much," Barry said. "You've got a lot of beard."

His father lay there quietly, his wasted arms at his sides.

"It's comforting," he said. "You'd be surprised how comforting it is."

Barry took up the razor, weighing it in his hand, rehearsing the angle at which he'd use it. He felt confident.

"If you have prayers to say . . ." he said.

"I've said a lot of prayers," his father answered.

Barry leaned over and placed the razor delicately against his father's face, setting the head accurately on the clean line near the ear where the long hair ended. He held the razor in the tips of his fingers and drew the blade sweetly through the lather. The new edge moved light as a touch over the hardness of the upper jaw and down to the angle of the chin, sliding away the bristles so easily that Barry could not feel their release. He sighed as he shook the razor in the hot water, washing away the soap.

"How's it going?" his father asked.

"No problem," Barry said. "You needn't worry."

It was as if he had never known what his father really looked like. He was discovering under his hands the clear bones of the face and head, they became sharp and recognizable under his fingers. When he moved his father's face a gentle inch to one side, he touched with his fingers the frail temples, the blue veins of his father's life. With infinite and meticulous care he took away the hair from his father's face.

"Now for your neck," he said. "We might as well do the job properly."

"You've got good hands," his father said. "You can trust those hands, they won't let you down."

Barry cradled his father's head in the crook of his left arm, so that the man could tilt back his head, exposing the throat. He brushed fresh lather under the chin and into the hollows alongside the stretched tendons. His father's throat was fleshless and vulnerable, his head was a hard weight on the boy's arm. Barry was filled with unreasoning protective love. He lifted the razor and began to shave.

"You don't have to worry," he said. "Not at all. Not about anything."

He held his father in the bend of his strong arm and they looked at each other. Their heads were very close.

"How old are you?" his father said.

"Seventeen," Barry said. "Near enough seventeen."

"You're young," his father said, "to have this happen."

"Not too young," Barry said. "I'm bigger than most men."

"I think you are," his father said.

He leaned his head tiredly against the boy's shoulder. He was without strength, his face was cold and smooth. He had let go all his authority, handed it over. He lay back on his pillow, knowing his weakness and his mortality, and looked at his son with wonder, with a curious humble pride.

"I won't worry then," he said. "About anything."

"There's no need," Barry said. "Why should you worry?"

He wiped his father's face clean of all soap with a damp towel. The smell of illness was everywhere, overpowering even the perfumed lather. Barry settled his father down and took away the shaving tools, putting them by with the same ceremonial precision with which he'd prepared them: the cleaned and glittering razor in its broken case; the soap, its bowl wiped and dried, on the shelf between the brush and the coronation mug; all free of taint. He washed his hands and scrubbed his nails. His hands were firm and broad, pink after their scrubbing. The fingers were short and strong, the little fingers slightly crooked, and soft, dark hair grew on the backs of his hands and his fingers just above the knuckles. Not long ago they had been small, bare hands, not very long ago.

Barry opened wide the bathroom window. Already, although it was not yet two o'clock, the sun was retreating and people were moving briskly, wrapped in their heavy coats against the cold that was to come. But now the window was full in the beam of the dying sunlight, and Barry stood there, illuminated in its golden warmth for a whole minute, knowing it would soon be gone.

Gamblers

On the hills outside the town, near the river and, further out, on the bleak moor, lie bundles of enormous masonry. The gaunt towers, the unlit, vaulting arches, the great walls of cut stone, are ruined and empty, their heavy margins flawed and irregular where parts have tumbled away. When I was a kid I used often to stand near a single fallen block, looking at it. It was a frowning gray, grass grew about its edges, a golden lichen furred its tiny crevices. Sometimes I'd climb on top of it, lie back, stare to the tops of the dark walls around, ominous, heavy, without purpose. I could not imagine any use for them at all. They were all that remained of the iron works which had been the reason for the town. I had never seen them working. Perhaps there were old men who had known this, perhaps they had worked there.

I used to wander often about the works, particularly on gloomy days when the sky had the color and something of the weight of those dull stone ruins and the rain beat without ceasing on those streaming walls. I knew the galleries, their floors covered with a soft dust of powdered limestone mortar, I had examined the cogwheels, taller than I was, rust-covered, much too heavy to think of shifting, that lay abandoned and broken against the walls of mills and cooling towers. It was in the works that I learned to fix a night line. One of the streams coming off the mountain had been channelled underground beneath a maze of ovens and engine rooms. It emerged just below the works, through a low tunnel. You could follow it, walking along a ledge of stone deep into the mountain, your hand on the exquisite, damp curve of the arched roof, until your nerve failed. I never went in far. Some people said there were rats in there. One warm day, sitting on the grass at the tunnel's mouth, I saw three trout swim out of the darkness. Easy and sinuous, they lay facing the current. The water was so clear that I could see their freckled colors, their red and black spots. An uncle of mine showed me how to set a night line. Every evening I'd get a few yards inside the tunnel, my baited hook ready, tie the line to a nail I'd hammered into the wall, lower the line gently into the water. A couple of lead shot about eighteen inches up from the hook kept the worm in an enticingly natural position. I've caught many a breakfast that way. But that was years later. The only other people to use the old works as much as I did were the gamblers.

There is a sense in which life itself was a gamble in our town. Hardly a man had work. In the whole length of our street, only two men could say they were employed, yet there was an air of urgency about the place, and a reckless, bitter gaiety. People kept busy. Many of them were serious gamblers; undeterred by lack of money, they could speak with authority of blood-lines and handicaps, were walking libraries of form, knew the idiosyncracies of all the race tracks in England, not one of which they had ever seen. They used to lay complex and intricate bets, trebles, accumulators, little side bets on the way, their ramifications causing hours of study and demanding a mastery of reckoning that accountants could envy, and all for an outlay of sixpence. Using matches for stakes, or perhaps cigarettes cut in halves, they would play card games of desperate intensity and skill. They searched for evidence of good fortune wherever they thought it could be found, in racing, in decks of cards, in the spin of a coin. The first gambler I knew was Owen Doherty.

The Dohertys lived near us, and Owen was the oldest of nine boys. He was shabby and elegant, walking slowly and straight-backed through the world, his thin, Irish face with its high cheekbones expressionless. I never saw Owen Doherty laugh at anything that was funny, although occasionally he'd give a high sharp bark of contempt at any opinion he thought particularly futile. He was much older than I, over twenty years older. I admired him because he was the best Pitch-and-Toss player in the district.

The young men used to play Pitch-and-Toss with pennies, or more probably halfpence, in a narrow lane behind the houses. I used to go down and watch them. From time to time, when I was very small, they'd send me away, since the game was illegal, liable to be interrupted by a patrolling policeman, and I at five or six would be a handicap to them and a source of information to the police. But I'd not gone far, continuing to watch from a tactful place higher up the lane.

The game was very simple. The boys used to take their coins between finger and thumb and aim them, with an underhand swing of the arm, at a mark about fifteen feet away. They used a small stone or a peg in the ground at which to aim. The player whose coin landed nearest the mark would collect the coins, place them on the flat of his hand, and toss them, glittering and spinning, into the air. A complicated system of heads and tails, which I never completely understood, decided the winner. Oh, to see Owen Doherty step up to the line, glare about him to demand the silence necessary for his total concentration, take the edge of his jacket in his left hand so that its drape should not impede his throw, lean forward, and sweetly aim! And later, as he placed the coins fastidiously along his palm and thin fingers, examining them so that their positions were absolutely right, holding them, waiting for the wind to die away before he threw them up, then we'd watch, knowing such artistry rare and sacred.

Only once did the police ever raid this game, as far as I know, and I was older then. I was at the head of the lane, bouncing a tennis ball on my right foot and counting aloud to see how many times I could manage it, when I heard yelps and shouts at the other end and the coin-tossers raced past me, going flat out. I looked down the lane and there was Sergeant Wilson, red-faced, pounding towards me at a frightening speed. I took off at once, despite my innocence, and had overtaken all the fleeing criminals long before they'd had time to scatter.

I turned right at the top of the lane, sped along Victoria Street and doubled back through Albert Road. Then I sat on our window sill, looking virtuous and innocent, as I had every right to. I wasn't even breathing hard. I was about fourteen then. This race was the cause of my graduating to the card games, hard, serious, for real money, that were held most nights in the old works.

Every boy in our town would have known the difference between a three of spades and a cup of tea at a very early age. I certainly did, but my knowledge stopped right there. For some reason I could never understand even the simplest card games. I would have been hard put to it to give a blind man reasonable exercise in a game of Snap and the satisfactions of Brag, Pontoon and Bridge have never been known to me. Yet that evening a couple of the older boys, together with Owen Doherty, came along to see me. I was teaching Muirhead, our cat, to jump through a hoop. She was refusing consistently, and mewing in a conciliatory manner. Pretty soon, I knew, she would bite and scratch. I was glad when the boys came up. They told me that I was just the fellow they wanted for their card school. Flattered but realistic, I told them that I couldn't play cards and that I had no money.

"No, no," said Owen. "We don't want you to play. We want you as lookout. The way you went past us this morning, there can't be a policeman in the force to live with you. What do you say? A shilling a week, for three evenings' work. Up at the old works."

We worked out a neat ploy. A disused railway track, its metal and sleepers long ago lifted to leave only the cinder ballast, led through the works, and I was to use it as a running track, supposedly training there while keeping a sharp lookout for policemen. Gareth Stephens had an old pair of shorts he'd grown too big for and he gave them to me. I liked them. They were of white silk, with blue lines around the waist and down the outside of the legs. Wearing these, a white vest and a pair of gym shoes, I began my employment, jogging along, practicing my starts, occasionally stopping for deep breathing and bending and stretching. I grew to like it very much. I trained sincerely, revelling in the increasing strength and stamina I began to recognize. I trained every night and on Saturday mornings. Forgotten were the card players, forgotten the plan by which, if the police ever came, I was to trot gently and inconspicuously towards the gamblers where they sat on stone benches under one of the great arches, warning them by whistling "The Last Round-up."

Even so, it should have been easy. Down before me, below the slope of the mountain, I could see the roofs of the town small and far away. There was no cover on the mountain, not a tree, not a bush. The scattered remnants of a few low stone walls, which had once contained the fields, the moor had long taken back and could certainly not have hidden a policeman. But nothing had happened for so long; I had been nearly two summers training in front of the works, and I had become unwary. I had become engrossed in my running, the running had taken over. So that one Friday evening, cloudless, in late July, I was suddenly astonished to see five stout blue bodies a couple of hundred yards away.

I turned and trotted back towards the works, prancing, knees high, shaking my arms as they hung limply at my side, as if to loosen the muscles. Behind my neck I thought I could feel the policemen mustering for a brief charge, and I could stand it no longer. I exploded into a frenzied sprint, all thought of "The Last Round-up" forgotten.

"Police! Police!" I hissed, whipping past the cavern like a short, white Jesse Owens. "Move, for Christ's sake!"

I kept on running until I was two hundred yards down the track, and then slowed gently to a walk, hands on hips, getting my breath. Then I turned and trotted back, breaking into fast sprints of twenty yards or so, straight out of the trot. I'd read about this in an old book by Jack Donaldson, who had been World Professional Champion in the days when shorts were worn below the knee. That book was a mine of information. It also had details of a high protein diet which was guaranteed to take a yard off your time, but I knew I'd never have the money for it. I raced past the empty arch. A policeman was bending down, collecting a scatter of cards that had fallen to the ground. The other four were looking up at the hillside. I could see the dark figures of the gamblers bucking like stags up the steep. Decorously, I slowed.

"Do you know them, boy?" said the policeman. "Do you know any of them?"

"Who do you mean?" I answered.

I shaded my eyes with my hand so that I could look more easily up the hill into the sunset. My friends were satisfactorily away.

The policeman sighed gently.

"Never mind," he said.

He stood looking at the cards in his hands.

"At least we gave them a fright," he said.

It was then that Mr. Everson appeared, stepping delicately over a huddle of stones at the fallen edge of a wall. Mr. Everson was a middle-aged gambler who sometimes sat in with my friends. He held in one hand a small bundle of plants and leaves and under his arm was a thick book with a respectable black cover.

"Good evening, gentlemen." he said. "And a very lovely evening too."

The policemen watched him as he came mildly down the track. They didn't answer.

"Look at these," said Mr. Everson, detaching a few dark green leaves from his miscellaneous bouquet. "The leaves of the wild violet, gentlemen, and here, a little late and therefore faded, the flower itself. A marvel, gentlemen, a marvel."

Mr. Everson chuckled with satisfaction over the fistful of flowers.

"It's astonishing," he said. "Don't you find it astonishing, to think that a mere fifty years ago the glare from these furnaces lit up the sky for miles around and nothing would grow on these hills because of the stench and fume of burning sulphur? And now, see, the violets are growing. Quite astonishing."

Mr. Everson held out his violets. Every time he said "astonishing," he opened wide his guileless eyes. It was quite a performance. A pair of ravens which lived high in the walls came out and croaked derisively, but the policemen said nothing. Mr. Everson walked through their silent suspicion.

"Come along, boy," he said. "You've done enough for one night. We don't want you to get stale."

I picked up my sweater and, side by side, we walked away. All the time I expected the policemen to call us back, but they didn't. Mr. Everson was perfectly calm, treating me with courtesy, as an equal. He was not only old, he was lame. He couldn't have run away with the others. When he was young he had injured his right knee playing football and the leg was permanently bent. Yet he walked strongly, taking a very short step off the right foot and gliding down in an immense long stride on his good leg. More excitingly, while he walked he grew tall and short in turn. On his injured leg his face was level with mine, but his left leg turned him into a tall man, a foot above me. So his voice soared and fell, too, as we walked into the town. He spoke to me about the wild flowers mainly. He knew all about them. He could outwit the police. He was a very clever man.

As I grew older my admiration for Laurence Everson grew too. We became friends, in spite of the difference in our ages. He was both intelligent and amusing, and in another place and at another time he could have done great things.

But in the waste and wilderness of our town he was able to cultivate only his individuality. He was well-read, scholarly even, and he belonged to several libraries. His interest in politics was informed and cynical, but he loved all kinds of sport. Whenever I'd call on him, I'd find him reading, his head resting on one hand, bent over his book. He always read at a table, sitting on a hard chair, the book fairly close to his face because he refused to wear glasses. It was a big face, large-featured, and he had flat lemon hair on top of his head, shading to gray around his ears. I didn't know he wore a wig until after his death, when one of his brothers told me.

Laurence was a fine snooker player and twice a week for years we played together. He taught me everything, from the basic grasp of the cue up. He taught me how to let the weight, the lead in the heavy base of the graduated wood, do the work, to bend low over the table so that the forward stroke would brush the knot of my tie, to use side and stop. From him I learned the correct bridge for every shot and to recognize a situation so clearly that I could carry in my mind not only the shot in hand but the next five or six shots. And we bet on every game we played during all that time, sometimes straightforward wagers based on a handicap which decreased as I improved, sometimes on some wild, surrealistic series of events which he improvised as we went along. Laurence Everson would bet on anything.

"Beautiful day," he'd say. "Bet you it will rain before two-thirty-three."

And we'd sit there, watching the second hand of our watches. Once we spent a whole afternoon betting in even pennies on his canary, a cinnamon-yellow Border that lived in the kitchen. First we bet on the precise second when it would sing and when that palled, we bet on the pitch of its first note, checking the result on Laurence's piano. This was the time he'd been ill and I'd gone in to see him. Mrs. Everson looked pale and anxious, but Laurence looked fine. He sat in an armchair, a rug about his knees, remarkably strong and imposing. He was sixty then.

After he recovered we went to Cardiff to see Glamorgan play Essex in the County Cricket Championship. We went by train and I won a few coppers on the journey, betting on the color of the shirt worn by the next man to enter our carriage. We were in plenty of time, found good seats and prepared to have a day of it. We couldn't have chosen better weather, hot enough to give the whole game a dreamlike clarity and yet comfortable enough for those of us who sat in our shirtsleeves.

In those days Glamorgan had an opening batsman named Smart, and he was very good. He played that day as if inspired and he'd scored fifty before lunch. Laurence and I ate our sandwiches and opened our bottles of beer. A couple of white pigeons fluttered on the grass in front of us, strutting for crumbs. We were perfectly contented. After the interval, Smart continued where he left off, playing shots of perfect timing and invention. Soon he was punching the ball all over the field. The Essex fast bowler, a youngster who never made the grade, suddenly dug one in so fiercely that it bounced head high and viciously, but Smart, leaning elegantly back, hooked it off his eyebrows. It was perfect. The ball came right at us and

Laurence, holding up a nonchalant hand, held it easily and tossed it back, laughing. A few people near us called and clapped and he turned around to say something. I could see his face, his amused eyes, and then it seemed to go to pieces, as if every muscle had suddenly snapped. He keeled right over and I held him as he was falling. God, he was a weight. People were helpful and competent. A doctor arrived within minutes and we got Laurence away to the hospital. He was quite unconscious and I stood around helplessly as they worked on him. It was his heart.

After a while he came to. He looked appalling. His skin, always sallow, was blue, and it seemed he could open only one eye.

"Did Smart get his hundred?" he whispered.

I could scarcely hear him.

"Yes," I said. I had no idea if it were true.

There was a long pause. I thought he'd lost consciousness again.

"Thank God for that," he said.

The doctor looked at me. He was a young man, perhaps a year or two older than I was. His white coat seemed a size too large for him and he looked cautious and sad.

"Your father?" he said.

"No," I said. "A friend. I've known him a long time, though."

"He's not good," said the doctor. "He's not at all well. I don't think he'll make it."

We were talking very quietly away from the bed, near the door. Laurence said something and I moved back to him.

"What time is it?" he asked.

I looked at my watch. It was four-thirty.

"Bet you," he said, "I'm still going at five o'clock."

He could barely speak.

"Done," I said. "Ten shillings."

That was an impossibly large bet for us.

"He's game," said the doctor. "By God, he's game."

We sat there for a long time listening to Laurence breathing. It seemed fainter and shallower. At last he spoke. He had no voice at all, but there was expression, somehow, in his terrible halting whisper. You could hear his amusement.

"Pay the wife," he said, "if I win."

He opened his eyes for the last time and I think he would have grinned had it been possible.

"Think of it," he said. "At last. At last one of us is on a dead cert."

I told all the boys that, and they all liked it, all those truthful and gallant gamblers. It was difficult to get Mrs. Everson to take the money, until I explained that it was a debt of honor, Laurence's last wager. She was a small, hard woman, very proud of Laurence.

"Gambling," she said tremulously. "It was his life."

A Professional
Man

Iwas not a willing soldier. At
eighteen I had too many things of my own to do, too many
places to go. I resented the idea of having my days ordered
for me, to wake to the bugle, to be known by a number, to
wear a uniform which made me indistinguishable from many
other young men. I had not long been aware of my individuality and found it exciting. Long avenues of time were open
before me and I wanted to explore them as I pleased. I was,
moreover, cynical about the great abstract concepts of patri-
otism and freedom. I was a surly conscript.

Yet the moment I walked inside the barracks that first afternoon I felt better. It was the sight of the coiled strands of spiked
wire secured to the top of the already high perimeter wall that
did it. They were so obviously mounted to keep soldiers inside
the barracks, not enemies out. This paradox made me understand at once that armies are comic institutions. I brightened,
I looked about with interest. With other young men I handed
in my papers, was allotted a space in a dormitory, marched
off to the dining hall.

Here we were given a meal of cold meat and bread and
butter. We sat at the long scrubbed boards and prepared to
eat. My neighbor, a heavy, red-faced Yorkshireman, stared at
his plate with suspicion. He turned it slowly around, bent

forward to inspect it at close range, leaned thoughtfully away from it.

"What's the matter?" I said.

"It's this meat," he said. He had a flat, cautious voice.

"What about it?" I said.

He turned upon me his brown, reproachful gaze.

"I can't recognize it," he said. He was serious and puzzled. "I'm a butcher. That's my trade, I know about meat. But I don't know what this stuff is. It's a bloody mystery."

I looked with more interest at my mystery.

"Heart?" I guessed helpfully, but my companion was not impressed.

"Well, pemmican," I said. But he did not listen.

We did not eat our meat, nor did the young men near us.

So began the mindless early days of our training. Our mornings were filled with repetitive drilling. We were very clumsy at first, but soon we marched and counter-marched in rhythmic complexities of accuracy across the barrack square. In the afternoons we performed some barren task or other, in the evenings we read, played cards, wrote letters. We weren't allowed into the little town. Life was boring.

Yet I enjoyed some of these physical things very much. I grew healthy and active. I ran long distances without distress, began to spend my free time in the gymnasium. The unvaried days passed without thought.

Occasionally we were given a job which had some purpose. When we had been soldiers for perhaps three weeks, I and seven of my fellows were set to wash down and clean three big transport trucks, large, square vehicles with canvas tops and sides, kept at the far end of the compound. The camp was not well defended there. Its boundary was no more than a fence of wire mesh five feet high, supported by concrete posts. A little grassy slope ran down to the fence and on the other side the visible free meadows stretched away, green and unhedged. Larks spun out of them, and, climbing perpendicularly, flung away their ecstatic notes. It was the first warm day of the year. The air was still and kind. We lolled on the grass, smoking, talking desultorily, drugged by sun. Our sergeant found us there. He was eloquent and angry. We stood at rigid attention while he blasted us, individually and as a group. He went on to point out that behavior like ours would inevitably prolong the war, might even be the cause of eventual, unthinkable defeat. All over the world, he snarled, our comrades were fighting in the hot dust of deserts and the squalor of jungles, their sacrifices counting as nothing as a result of our irresponsibility.

"Now," he said, "you are all young. You get one more chance. I shall be gone an hour, and when I come back these vehicles will be shining. Do you understand, glittering! There will not be the suspicion of a speck of dust within ten yards of them. Move! Move!"

We moved. We shot to the hoses, the buckets and brushes. The sergeant called me back.

"You," he said, "I've been watching you. You've got a very nasty attitude, a very cynical attitude."

"Yes, Sergeant," I said, stunned.

"You want to put your back in it," he said. "You'll never get on otherwise. So watch your step when I'm around."

"Yes, Sergeant," I said.

The next morning a small, important corporal came into the dormitory and called my name.

"042 Graham?" he said. "That you? Report to the adjutant at once. Jump to it."

There was a sharp intake of breath from my contemporaries, who imagined me guilty of some enormous crime. The corporal, gratified, bustled off.

The adjutant was a heavy man, wearing a shy attempt at a military moustache. In civilian life he was a lawyer.

"Ah, Graham," he said, "at ease, Graham."

He shuffled the papers on his desk.

"We've been looking through your records," he said. "The records of all you new men. To see where you might be best placed after your initial training, where you might best serve the army."

He smiled, man to man.

"It seems, Graham," he said, "you're a well-educated boy. Did well at school, destined for university."

"Yes sir," I said.

His breathing was so noisy I thought he must have asthma.

109

"Ah," he said, "well done. Why don't you try for a commission? Apply for entry to an Officers' Training Unit? We're always looking for keen, alert men, with the right background."

"I've not thought of it, sir," I said.

"Think of it now," he said. "Here you are at the start of what could be a splendid career, splendid."

"I'd like that," I said. I would have agreed to almost anything for a change of scene.

"Good man," he said. "Good man, well done. We'll send your papers off as soon as we can."

I went out of the office. My squad was drilling with others; perfectly, line by line, in faultless step, like metronomes they marched and wheeled and crossed, their loud heels falling as one on the tarmac, their arms swinging in unison, their faces so many white anonymous ovals. I did not want to be one of them. Walking away, I savored my momentary freedom. The gym was empty. I changed and as I laced my shoes I sang, my voice echoing off the high glass roof. I dragged the vaulting horse into the middle of the floor, placed a springboard in front of it, walked away. I turned at the far wall, took a deep breath, and raced along the boards. I hit the springboard hard and soared in a leap of spectacular celebration over the horse. I landed wrongly and broke my ankle. I thought I heard it snap.

The break didn't knit, despite my youth and health. Eventually the doctors fastened a metal plate to the reluctant bone, reset my lower leg in plaster and sent me to hospital to convalesce. I went in an ambulance, with a medical orderly as escort.

The hospital was on the outskirts of a Midland town which had been, when such places were fashionable, a popular spa. Victorian ladies and gentlemen had come to spend some time there, to drink the natural waters, redolent of sulphur, which were said to be specific cures for many illnesses. A whole service industry had sprung up about these visitors, and although the place was much less popular, remnants of the tradition remained. The town was rich in eating houses and tea rooms, had many boarding houses and hotels. The hospital to which I was sent was itself a hotel in peacetime, the largest of the hotels. It stood on a hill above the town, like a castle grown domestic and benevolent. We broken soldiers lived there in luxury, two to a room. We were there to allow our bones time to heal properly. There were men among us who had been injured in spectacular accidents, in bad landings by parachute, falls from cliffs while training as commandos, violent crashes on motorcycles. They had long boards positioned to keep their spines and necks rigid, their arms were supported at shoulder height on curious platforms, they walked crablike along the gracious corridors. Lame and cheerful, we ate in the elegant dining room, relaxed in lounges designed to comfort the excesses of an earlier generation. The weather was good, the hills open. Once the surgeons had paid us their morning calls the days were normally ours.

Those of us not able to leave the hospital grounds would play bowls on the green in front of the building, or a kind of cripples' tennis on the hard courts; but there were daring and lively men who would not be handicapped by their injuries, who were adventurous to the point of recklessness, and they went wider afield. I, with my small fracture, often joined them. We sometimes hired ponies from a nearby stables. Clambering into the worn saddles, we'd gallop through the streets of the little town, legs sticking out at grotesque angles, our stiff bodies jolting up and down. After an exploit like this I'd return to the hospital and tell my roommate, Alastair Ball, what we had been doing. Alastair was one of the few injured still confined to bed. He lay there, his legs trapped in a web of ropes and pulleys, and he was unruffled, tolerant, amiable all day long. He was twenty years old.

I had never met anyone remotely like Alastair. He was rich, he had been to a famous school, he was enormously well informed. He spoke French and German. I had never left the country, but Alastair had lived in Europe—his father was a diplomat—had visited India. His speech, slow, calm, assured, was quite unlike my hurried and tentative sentences. He spoke to me in the evenings of politics, finance, economics. His cold passion for mathematics almost convinced me of its clear beauty. I began to read the books Alastair loaned me, to listen to the music he chose to hear on the radio. In return I gave him full accounts of the events of the day as I saw them out-side our room. The war was distant and unreal. I never thought of it.

At last Alastair was allowed out of bed. First on crutches and then with the help of a stick, he walked to the bathroom, to change his library books, to meals. The first time I saw him upright I was astonished. He was a very tall man, easily six feet four inches. As he grew stronger he began to walk the halls and corridors of our ornate hospital, his stick sharp on the tiled floors. I spent a lot of time with him then. On fine days we would be out on the terrace, moving gravely on our incompe-tent legs, talking, always talking.

Our first journey outside the hospital grounds was to the town. We sauntered to the bus stop in the August sunshine, happy in our recovering strength, carefree. Alastair was explain-ing to me the complexities of the Stock Exchange, but I wasn't listening too hard. I knew I would go through life allowing the accidents and coincidences of small days to take me with them. The Stock Exchange was not for me. I had no idea of what I could do, what I wanted to do. It was enough to sit in the bus in the summer heat, smiling as the bus swung around corners, past the rough limestone walls which hedged the fields, rolling downhill to the shops and houses. We got off at the station and two blue butterflies, perhaps the Holly Blue, danced in front of us all the way to the river bridge.

I loved the river bridge. I always stopped there, to lean on the stone parapet. The river, an exquisite chalk stream, formed a deep pool under the bridge, its flow so imperceptible it could be still, its clarity unflawed so you saw every detail, the polished ledges which formed the washed sides of the channel, the min-ute viridian ferns lodged in crannies, the slate-colored river bed. One bank was a face of stone which reached the bridge itself, and the other was lower, no more than a foot above the water. A grassy area led down to it, bordered with wildflowers and marigolds. Small tables were standing on the neat lawn and people sat there, drinking coffee. Some rowing boats were tied up at the bank, substantial boats for so small a river. Seven of our friends were attempting to climb into the nearest of them.

It was a difficult business organizing their limbs into so narrow a space. Laughing, hauling and shoving, they dragged each other about until they were all, somehow, seated and they began to move into midstream. From above, the boat and its wild oars looked like an insect, a great beetle many-legged and bristling, which had fallen into the water and having no idea where land was, paddled aimlessly on the surface. As I thought this, someone lost an oar, leaned precariously for it, and almost toppled out of the boat. At once the craft's uncertain balance was spoiled; it started to totter, to rock, it sent waves across the smoothness of the pool and then, as if it had a malevolent life of its own, it spilled its shouting crew into twelve feet of water. They sank with such grace it seemed the river might almost have supported them. Their lamed clumsiness, their plaster heaviness vanished from them. Turning slowly in the dreaming passages of the water, they were almost fragile as they drifted through the pure and silent element. We saw them reach the bed of the river and push again for the surface and then, with others, we moved to help them, holding to them long poles ready at the water's edge, throwing them life-belts, bringing them red-faced and dripping to the river bank. The whole action was so beautiful and so funny that none of us, rescued or rescuers, thought once of danger or possible tragedy. The squelching soldiers hired a taxi and drove in triumph to the hospital. Alastair and I had lunch in town, visited the bookshop, went back up the hill in the afternoon bus. When I got in my doctor told me that I would never have more than one-third movement in my ankle and I was to be discharged from the army.

That was a day early in the week, Monday or Tuesday. The following Friday, wearing a civilian suit, I walked down the hill to catch the London train. My career in the army was over. Alastair had given me one of his walking sticks, a Malacca, light brown in color. It was too long for me, of course. I had to cut it down. I had said goodbye to men I had known for a few months, promised to write to them. I didn't write. That was forty years ago. I learned to manage my stiff ankle, it's not been difficult. I have some arthritis in it now.

It is an irony that I, who had no sense of direction as a young man and drifted with the wind, should have spent all my life since then in one profession, almost in one place. Directly from the army I went to the university. I was utterly at home. I took my degree and was appointed to teach at another university. I've been there ever since. It's been an uneventful life, but satisfying. My misgivings, my restlessness, have been small. I've specialized in Anglo-Saxon and Early English Literature and published a little work in the field. I have not been unsuccessful. In recent years I've become interested in Norwegian poetry of the Romantic period, the work of men like Wergeland and Johan Sebastian Welhaven. I've translated some of this work, but my resources are limited, my knowledge of the language insufficient. Last month, when a chance opportunity arose for me to visit the university at Bergen I accepted at once.

It didn't work too well. I had been loaned an apartment in a house where all the tenants were professors and were away for the summer. I was very solitary. The long daylight bothered me. I never grew accustomed to the gray hours filling the streets long after I expected darkness. It was colder, too, than I had anticipated. It took time to get used to the place, to accept its northern face, to hear its voices. Each day I walked down to the waterfront, past the fishmarket, along the north wall of the harbor, back again. It was better when I started going to the university.

I had there the use of a small office and a typewriter. The library was open and the young librarian very helpful, although he couldn't understand my interest in these "small men," as he called them. I worked there for a week, arriving each day about eight-thirty, leaving at six in the afternoon, eating my lunch of bread and fruit in the office. I made some headway. One lunch-time I decided to go down to the harbor and buy some fish. Bergen is a great fish market and I had seen the boats come in with staggering hauls, mainly cod, but some hake and haddock. Mackerel too, and once a giant salmon, well over sixty pounds, taken silver and glittering out of the green sea.

I waited in the short queue, bought my cutlets, and turned sharply into the man behind me. What happened was entirely involuntary, much quicker than recognition, something instinctive.

"Alastair?" I said. "Alastair Ball?"

The tall man bent his head down towards me and said something in Norwegian. He was a man in late middle age, the hair below his hat gray. He wore a light raincoat.

"I'm sorry," I said, "I don't speak Norwegian."

"Ah, you English," he said. "Insular, insular English. You should learn our language. It's not difficult. But *Britannia insula est*—that was the first sentence in my Latin primer and it is a true sentence."

He beamed down at me, a mild face, a solicitous face.

"I mistook you for someone I knew," I said.

"A friend?" he said. "You have a friend who looks like me? Very likely. I am a typical Norwegian, a Viking, you know? Well, just let me buy my supper and I will see if I know your friend."

His English was noticeably accented, if clear and fluent. He turned to the fishmonger and afterwards we walked together past the old building which had been the dwellings and offices of the merchants of the Hanseatic League. It is preserved now as a museum. I had been inside. I told the tall man my name and what I was doing in the city.

"So," he said. "Very good. It is time someone took a little notice of us. Please let me introduce myself. I am Jens Edwardsen, a businessman of this place, but I have some culture, I am interested in painting, music, some literature. Welhaven, eh?"

He stopped in front of me and began to chant, marking the rhythm with his right hand, like a conductor.

"*Lydt gjennem Luften in Natten farer*
et Tog pas skummende sorte Heste.
I Stormgang drage de vilde skarer;
de have kun Skyer til Fodefaeste—

"What do you make of that? That's 'Welhaven.' What would you call that in English, 'The Wild Hunt,' perhaps? Isn't that very good?'' He took off his glasses and laughed aloud. I began to like him very much.

"And now my friend," he said, "I must return to my office. We must work, you know, work will not wait for us. But perhaps you will be kind enough to have dinner with me this evening, shall we say at six o'clock, and afterwards we will go and hear some organ music. If you like organ music, that is."

I was glad to have talked to him. The whole day seemed more cheerful. I walked through the center of the city and for the first time thought it beautiful. I did not see the relative unattractiveness of the shops, did not object to the cold and choppy waters of the fjord. A fitful sun shone on the old fort of Fredriksburg.

We ate at an Indian restaurant and afterwards walked to Johannes Kirken, where a Dutch organist played a program of music by Bach, Buxtehude, Couperin and Cesar Franck. The organ was superb and the performer excellent, but the church was no more than half full. We came out into the long summer twilight of Norway, walked through the parks and squares not saying much, at ease. About ten-thirty we sat on a bench near the Bergenhus, the palace of the Norwegian kings in the Middle Ages. Edwardsen lit his pipe and looked out over the roofs.

"I am interested to find out," he said, "who this friend can be, the man you thought was I."

"Oh," I said, "it was a stupid mistake. It was someone I knew many years ago, when we were very young. It was just your height, I was startled by your height, your outline."

Four or five magpies walked impertinently in front of us. I had never seen so many magpies as there were in Bergen, in the parks, in the streets, on the roofs of houses. In England they are country birds, sleek and immaculate; but in Bergen they are everywhere, raffish scavengers. Years ago, during the war, I thought they flew like bombers, Dorniers maybe, with their long tails.

"So," said Edwardsen, "he was a tall man, your friend? You were young men together? Youth is a time of great friendships, I think. But his face was not at all like mine, I would hope."

He took off his hat and his glasses and stared at me earnestly. There he sat, turned towards me, his hair gray, his face lined, his long hands quiet on his knees.

"No," I said, "not at all like yours."

He smiled, his eyes mischievous and teasing.

"Are you sure," he said, "Private Graham?"

And then I knew that my instinct had not been at fault, that behind the face of the sixty-year-old man Alastair Ball was alive. I recognised then the bones of his face, the shape of his hair, and in a few moments I saw the young man appear.

"But why, Alastair?" I said.

He told me. He was a genuine merchant of the town of Bergen, had been since 1945 when he had appeared there from Oslo with all his documents perfect. He had a circle of old friends, he was successful, comfortably off. I didn't understand.

"Can't you guess?" he said. "I'm a collector of information. I sit here and do business with men of many countries. I am near many frontiers, Germany, Poland, Russia. I travel. People come to see me."

"You're a spy," I said.

"A professional man," he said, speaking with his old, languid, English voice, "with a perfect cover until you came along, bawling out a forgotten name to all and sundry."

He grinned, and I with him.

"I shan't say anything," I said.

"More than that," he said, "we won't meet again. And if we see each other in the street we won't even say hello."

"Was it chance," I said, "that I bumped into you in the fish market?"

"Pure chance," he said, "one of the hazards we can't guard against."

He stood up and stretched. I saw then that he really was an elderly man.

"How do you know I can be trusted?" I said.

He looked at me over his glasses.

"The wires have been busy," he said, "between here and London this afternoon. I've had your whole life in front of me since four o'clock. Blameless and trustworthy, that's you."

"And if I hadn't been," I said.

He gestured impatiently towards the waters of the sea.

"It's a rough game," he said. "Be glad you don't belong to it. Goodbye, I've always wanted to know what happened to you. I'm glad all has gone well."

He turned away and walked down the slope, an erect figure, very tall, unswerving.

"Mr. Edwardsen," I called, "I still have that walking stick."

He flapped a hand, in acknowledgement or dismissal, but did not turn around. I let him go out of sight and waited fifteen minutes more. Walking alone through the empty streets I came upon a small memorial stone, to a boy who had been a messenger in the underground movement during the war. The Germans had shot him. Before I reached my apartment I found two more. I had not seen them before. I had not been looking for them.

Lurchers

.

When my great-grandfather
came out of the hills above Llandovery in 1864, his furniture
on a flat cart, his pans in clanking bundles, his pots in wicker
baskets, his two small boys kicking their legs over the back-
board, you can be sure he brought his dogs with him. He was
not migrating very far—not more than fifty miles—but he was
leaving behind the green, Welsh-speaking country in which
he had been born. He never went back. He walked with his
wife at the mare's head through the hamlets of Halfway and
Llywel, and his cousins the Gardners ran out to wish them luck
and to give them parting gifts—small lustre jugs, packets of tea.
Reaching Sennybridge, they turned south to climb the gaunt
and sneering heights of the Brecon Beacons. Here the little boys
climbed down to lighten the load as, dwarfed by height,
silenced by darkness, the family crawled for hours under black
Fan Frynach before they reached the top of the pass at the
Storey Arms Inn. Then they could see below them the spoiled
valleys of Glamorgan, their sides already pocked with the
heaped detritus of the Industrial Revolution, their skies lit by
leaping flames from the furnaces or hidden by rolling smoke.

Yes, my great-grandfather brought the dogs. He needed
them. He was not going to the foundries or the coal mines but
to a farm on the clear hills above the newly smoking town.
He would have a white house, thick-walled, four-square to the

winds; he would have an enclosure of over forty acres and graz-
ing rights on twelve long miles of open mountain. On those
high, unhindered moors he would raise his sheep—not your
demure symbols of meekness, all soft fleece and gentle bleat-
ing, but stubborn, short-tempered animals, malevolent and cunning, able to grow stout on the shortest grass, yellow-eyed as
goats, fluent as goats on the rock faces. They could outrun the
mountain fox, they could lie snug for days under a fall of snow
in the hollow, fetid caves of their own warm breathing.

To contain such animals without dogs would have been
impossible. They would have been among my great-
grandfather's most valued possessions—more prized than the
corner cupboard given to him by his mother, more valuable
than the dresser and the six oak dining chairs made for him
by Jonah Jenkins of Trecastle. He needed his dogs more than
he needed the tough brown mare that pulled the cart. Without them he could not have commanded the long slab of the
mountain, acres of sloping turf and bracken on which his sheep
were to feed, he could not have stood alone and calm while
the dogs worked above him, extensions of his will. Each obedient to its own set of signals, his sheepdogs ran, crouched,
sidled, and slunk close, and faultlessly gathered in his butting
and recalcitrant animals. Panting, they brought in the sheep
for lambing and dipping and marking, they held and penned
them for shearing, they cut out the sick and injured so that
my great-grandfather could treat them with his homemade
drenches and salves. And after his death, in my grandfather's
day, the descendants of those dogs still ran the hills, hard,
strong, heavy-coated, their names repeated generation after
generation: Bob, Gyp, Mot, Fan, Meg, Dick, Carl—
monosyllables easy to shout against the wind.

They were the strong aristocrats of the farm, moving stiff-
legged and contemptuous through the yard, scattering the silly
buff Orphington and Light Sussex fowl my grandfather so
admired, or sleeping thin-eyed in a patch of sun by the barn.
They lived only for my grandfather, they had no existence without him. When he appeared around the dim back door and
walked down the path, they swung in behind him, heads low,
waiting only for the twitch of his hand to send them racing

for the flocks. Wherever he went, two or three dogs padded silently behind him, as natural as his shadow. They were as close to him as his hands.

On warm afternoons we would sit together, old man and boy, talking. We spoke with wonder of the world outside the farm, for we shared an ignorance of that community which did not live directly, as we did, by what it produced. We believed completely that the rest of society was in some sense an immoral growth, a parasite like mistletoe, hanging without purpose from the great oak of our work. At such times we would look with pride at our dogs, seeing them as symbols of those puritan qualities we admired; they were staunch, loyal, infinitely hardworking, shy—like us—and sometimes sullen with strangers. And yet, although I loved my grandfather's sheepdogs and could work Bob myself, I did not want one of my own. I yearned for another kind of dog altogether—a long, silent hunter, a dog outside the law. I wanted a lurcher.

Sometimes a group of men—small men, dark, wary-eyed—would move through our big field on the way to the mountain. Beyond a nod in our direction, or a muttered good morning, they rarely greeted us. They were gypsies. They would have with them four or five lurchers, a kind of dog unchanged since the time of the pharaohs, with the lines of greyhounds but quieter, more secretive. Most of them would have long hair. They were bred from working greyhounds, with an occasional cross of sheepdog or, sometimes, deerhound blood. They were beautiful. It was their sheepdog ancestry that enabled them to hunt silently, that made them hardy and resourceful, and instantly obedient, despite the raging instinct of the chase which came from the greyhound.

My grandfather would stand unspeaking, rigid with distaste, when such a little group crossed our ground. The gypsies would climb the stile and cross the railway line, the gray dogs would wind themselves sinuously through the wire or, effortlessly, without fuss, leap the fence. When the men had vanished, quietly with their quiet dogs, my grandfather would turn away, two sharp, unaccustomed spots of color on his cheekbones, his mouth stern beneath his white mustache. He was a short, generally smiling man, extravagantly generous.

He could whistle like a thrush. He knew where the early flowers grew, the windflower and the primrose, and where the mistle thrush, first of birds to nest, kept her spotted eggs. He never seemed to hurry. His speech was slow and quiet. But his rare anger was terrible. He hated lurchers—I could see that. I dared not ask him for one—though I wanted one of those lean outlaws far more than respectability—because I had no wish to set my grandfather's violence alight.

Still, once the old man had turned away, I would follow the gypsies at a timid distance. Standing in the shadow of a clump of stubby hawthorn, or almost hidden in bracken waist-high to a man, I would watch the hills for the lurchers—long, slim as stems, powerful, coursing and turning the blue hares of the mountain. I stood one morning in the red ferns, powder of winter frost unthawed on every brittle frond, when a tall lurcher stopped in front of me. I saw its eyes. They were large and gentle, curiously distant and impersonal. It opened its mouth in a kind of laugh, and I had a glimpse of the terrifying white teeth before it was whistled away and I ran downhill, frightened and elated, in the thin tracks made by the sheep. A lurcher can pull down a grown deer. According to record, in Cowdray Park, in Sussex, in the summer of 1591, Queen Elizabeth saw "sixteen bucks, all having fair play, pulled down after dinner" by dogs very much like these lurchers.

Too soon, we had to leave the farm. We went to live at the edge of town, in a row of houses almost where the fields began, and every day my grandfather walked out into the country, smiling as best he could, and wrecked by age. Of our dogs we took only Bob with us. The big orange and white sheepdog, dignified and brilliantly handsome, was too old to work with a new master. He settled down well, sat mildly on our front lawn, was gentle with passing children. He lived a long time, dying when I was seventeen, a year or two older than he was. It was June, and we buried him in the garden and planted a cherry tree over him.

That summer I found a holiday job in a fruit-and-vegetable warehouse. I used to rise early and walk through the streets as the summer dawn gradually brought the town awake. I used to hump boxes of fruit onto the trucks for delivery to shops all down the valley. I liked it very much. On Saturdays I used to work right through to late afternoon, loading up, checking invoices and delivery notes, taking new deliveries from the growers, and then I'd get paid. I had never known such wealth. The whole world grew docile and manageable under the power of the three pound notes I carried away each Saturday. Whole perfumed empires opened up for my inspection—cafes, theatres, gentlemen's outfits with real silk ties. It was a heady time. On my last Saturday Mr. Frimpton put three pounds into my hand, and then, with a light smile, two more. "You've been a good lad," he said. "Buy yourself something special."

That evening I went alone to swim in the river. September was already chilling the water, but it seemed warmer when the sun had gone down. It was my last freedom before school began again, and it was fine to be there, washing summer off my summer skin, lazing softly downstream. I got out in the dusk, as the bats were beginning to fly, and walked down the lane for home. A ghost of the moon was out in a sky still full of daylight. Long grass in the hedgerows was ripe and heavy, there was a faint odor of hay as the dew settled.

Three people were standing in the lane, and one of them was singing. The singer was Talbot Hamer, famous in our town as an outrageous firebrand, a drinker and a fighter. He sang with his head slightly raised and his arms at shoulder height in front of him, palms upward as if he held on his hands the airy weight of his lovely voice. He was singing "The Last Rose of Summer," and he was not drunk. His two companions, men of his own age—thirty, perhaps—were listening seriously, and Talbot filled the lane with his perfect singing, as a river fills its bed.

"All her lovely companions," sang Talbot Hamer, "are faded and gone." It was unbearably beautiful. We waited until the final note, sweet and poignant beyond our understanding, had died in the darkening lane. Talbot stood there smiling down at us, amused at our stillness.

"I didn't know you'd gone in for singing, Talbot," said one of the men.

"I have," said Talbot, nodding dreamily, still aware of the song inside his head. "I've been taking lessons for two years now."

The music still held us, a sense quieter and more intense than silence. We stood there respectfully, not knowing what to do.

"Do you want to buy a dog?" said the other man at last, looking at me.

It was as if I were being asked to take part in a ceremony of gratitude. I looked at the long, pale dog standing at the man's knees.

"He's a good one," said Talbot Hamer. The spell of his song was with him; he looked at the evening with an exalted eye.

"Yes," I said. "I'll buy him."

"Two pounds," the man said.

I took the two carefree pounds Mr. Frimpton had given me and handed them over. The man put them in his pocket without a glance. "He'll catch anything that moves," the man said. "Retrieve to hand. Gentle, obedient. I'd not sell him to anyone but you."

"I believe you," I said.

He handed over the dog's leash. The whole affair was so tenuous that I was startled by the weight and touch of the leash; it was heavy, smooth and heavy—real saddler's leather, and hand-stitched. It was pliable and slightly oily with use, about eighteen inches long, and fastened by a spring clip to the dog's wide collar.

"I'll take him, then," I said.

The men stood aside and I walked past them, the dog going with me, unprotesting. He didn't look back.

"The name's Ben," the man called. "He's a good one, mind. You look after him and he'll look after you."

I trotted away as Talbot Hamer sang again. *"Una furtiva lagrima,"* he sang. *"Negl' occhi suoi spunto: quelle festose giovani . . ."*

I turned the corner and could hear him no more.

I took Ben into the house and had a look at him. He was bigger than I'd thought—all of twenty-nine inches at the shoulder—and rough-coated. He was mostly white, but there were patches of orange on his body—on the ribs and the right shoulder—and his ears were deep orange, almost red. He might have been two years old. I fed him in the kitchen—a bowl of crusts softened in milk. He ate thoroughly, carefully cleaning every particle of food from the dish, and then looked thoughtfully about him. His expression was both cynical and mournful, and he never looked any different all the years I had him. That's how I came to own my first lurcher.

Talbot Hamer was quite right; the dog was a good one. When he was with us, he was vastly obedient, without ever letting us believe that he was at all humble or subservient; he followed at our heels, alert for any order. But he was also independent, roaming the town at will. I often saw him swinging down the High Street with his long, economical stride— deep-ribbed, solitary, detached from the scene, as if he were some thoughtful philosopher engrossed in a profoundly satisfying problem. On such occasions he did not seem to recognize me; he looked away tactfully, as if to let me know that he was his own man with his own concerns. He roamed very far afield. Men from outlying villages, seeing him with me, would often come up and tell me of his exploits in their parishes, for he was a famous lover, visiting for miles around.

He was also very fond of beer. He was at his best in small inns on winter evenings, when the talk was good. His method was a simple one, I was told. He would sidle in quietly, offering a token wag of the tail if anyone looked at him, sigh gently, and lie down out of the way in some corner. His eyes would grow soft as he looked beyond the walls at some distant and innocent memory. In a little while everybody would forget all about him. The old drinkers sat on their benches, laughed, pulled at their beer, wiped the foam from their mouths, and put their mugs on the floor, the better to illustrate a point in some hot debate. Casually, Ben would saunter over and join the group, stretching almost invisibly in the shadow of a bench or a chair. And then, dreamily and in complete silence, he would lap up the beer. Men who knew him would chase him out the moment his long head appeared around the inn door, and he often had to move very smartly. On the other hand, he also managed to drink a lot of beer.

He was wonderful in the country, an incomparable crafts-man. He and I worked together. A little shift of his head would lead me unerringly to some animal—a hedgehog, maybe, curled up in his leaves and just about to stir, or a bird. I had never seen a snipe until Ben turned one out for me one heavy winter morning when the ground was hard and the only place for such shy creatures was on the softness at the edge of a stream. Ben held back, looking to make sure I was attending, and then moved noiselessly into the willows. At once, a snipe came rocketing out, breaking into erratic flight, uttering two stiff cries. Ben looked at me sardonically and then stretched his long body in a gallop over the frozen meadow. He was a hunter all his life, he could not be kept from hare or game bird. Well, that was long ago. Talbot Hamer is dead, the summer of his voice a memory.

The most beautiful lurcher I ever saw was Georgie Todd's Dagger—a spectacular, golden dog Georgie owned when I first knew him, about fifteen years back. Oh, he was lovely, a great beauty, over seventy pounds in weight, and he moved like this-tledown. His yellow coat was harsh to the touch, his eyes were dark and kind. He and Georgie were very like each other—large, quiet, diffident, and very gentle.

Georgie has a fruit farm the other side of the Downs, toward Pulborough. He grows apples mainly—Bramley's, Cox's, russets—but he has a few pear trees and a couple of acres of strawberries. The house is an old Georgian farmhouse, sim-ply and beautifully preserved. The furniture is good, too, each piece shrewdly chosen. Georgie and his wife had taken great pains over it, bought carefully over the years, and have never been impulsive or haphazard. I always thought it strange that so neat and methodical a pair as Georgie and Phyllis Todd should have a dog at all, even one as striking as Dagger.

Their greatest enthusiasm is for the history of this part of Sussex—the Weald and the South Downs—and they are very serious about it, very knowledgeable. Between them, they've done some first-class research; Georgie does the field work, and Phyllis, a meticulous woman, looks after records and docu-ments. Dagger was very much Georgie's dog. Without being in any way unkind, Phyllis seemed hardly aware that the animal was about. One day, in the Welldigger's Arms at lunchtime, looking at Dagger as he lay at our feet, I asked Georgie to sell me the dog.

"I shan't sell him," Georgie said. "We get along very nicely; he's a sweet old dog."

"Where did you buy him, Georgie?" I said.

"I didn't buy him," Georgie said.

He told me how, three years before, he had been walking down Bury Hill. It was a day of quite exceptional heat, after a succession of very hot days. Georgie had got up in the cool of the morning and tramped off to visit a church in one of the villages; he was tracing the ramifications of an old local family and had gone to look at the gravestones in the churchyard. Now, in the late morning, the heat was growing intense. Traffic wasn't as heavy in those days, and you could walk the roads with pleasure, but that day the dust was everywhere—chalk dust off the Downs, very thick, like powder. It rose in little puffs as Georgie plodded down the hill, getting into his nose and throat, making him think of the long, cool drink he'd have when he reached home. He sat on a stone at the side of the road to watch a gypsy caravan, pulled by a bay mare, climbing the hill toward him. It was a barrel caravan, its canvas stretched neatly over its hooped ribs, and it was in good shape, but the mare was finding the going hard; she was distressed and blowing as she dug into the steep of the hill. A thin young man walked with her, a surly young man, lean and dark in the face. They came slowly by, the caravan heavily laden, well down on its two creaking springs.

"You've got a load on," said Georgie, smiling.

The man didn't lift his head. George stood up. At the tail of the caravan, tied to a spar by a rope heavy enough to hold a lion, was a lurcher puppy. He tottered and swayed, yelping each time he was dragged by the neck as the mare pulled gamely on. He was so dirty that Georgie could not guess at his color. He was far gone. Georgie, surprised by his own anger, ran to the front of the van.

"Do something about the dog!" he shouted. "You're killing him!"

Very quietly and deliberately the young gypsy led his mare to the roadside grass and dropped the reins over her head. She stood there, exhausted. The man said nothing at all. He took from his pocket a black-handled clasp knife and opened it with his thumbnail. The blade was long and glittering, thin with use and viciously sharp. Georgie knew that his last moments had come and prepared to meet his death as well as he could. All he could think of, he told me, smiling, was to stand erect and die bravely. But the gypsy walked slowly past him, down the side of the van, disappeared around the tail. The puppy began to scream, and Georgie's quick relief turned to indignation.

"My God," he thought, starting to run after the man, "he's going to kill the dog." But then the young man came back toward him, in one hand the open knife and in the other the heavy rope, its fibers freshly cut. The dog, unhurt, howled at the other end. The young man bent down and lifted the animal, holding it to Georgie. "Take it," he said. "Take it away." His voice was thick and trembling, as if he held his violence in check only by the severest effort.

"That was the first time I saw his face clearly," said Georgie. "The man was desperate, and I became even more frightened. I still believe that if I hadn't taken the dog—well, the fellow would have knifed me. I grabbed the pup and ran downhill as fast as I could go."

Georgie carried the dog home and, in time and with patience, turned him into Dagger. He was a lovely dog, noble and unassuming. After his death Georgie never had another.

There's a parti-colored dog that lives on the coast road with an old gypsy couple. I saw this dog when it was a sapling, running loose on Clymping beach, and I followed it home. The old man was sitting on the step of his caravan, a wooden van, traditionally painted. The old people travel the road from Littlehampton to Portsmouth and back again. I often see them parked on some small plot of grass, their skewbald gelding hobbled close by.

"That's a nice dog," I said to the old man.

"He'll come," said the old man. "In time, he'll come."

"What's his name?" I said.

"Toro," said the old man. "It's a good name. You should always give a dog a name he can grow up to. I've had three dogs named Toro in my life, and they've all been good. Belle is a good name, too."

The old man would not live well without Toro. There will not be many nights when the dog will not be silently quartering some rich man's fields, bringing almost apologetically to the pot the fresh spoils of the countryside—hare, rabbit, a pheasant so gently killed that the bronze feathers are not displaced.

The lurcher I have now, Jess, came to me from the dogs' home when she was twelve weeks old—a pathetic little waif, very ugly and awkward. But you could tell she'd be elegant; the length was already apparent in leg and back. At that time she couldn't manage herself at all well. Even her slight weight was sometimes too much for her, and she'd slowly collapse, spread-eagled, unable to rise and yelling with pain. At first we couldn't give her enough food—she ate all day long—and as she grew stronger she began to forage for herself. A poor sparrow once flew into the garden wall. It had hardly fallen to the ground when she'd swallowed it at a gulp. She began to catch wood pigeons. Slow to get up the birds would be, in their first clatter of flying, and she would grab one of them and, running on, take it to corner of the field. Later I'd find two small pink feet—all that would be left of Jess' meal. But she's big now, a sturdy animal, full of grace and power.

I know quite a lot about her—where she was bred, her parentage, her precise age. When she was about twelve months and beginning to look as she should, I had her out on the lawn, chasing a ball. A young man came over and leaned on the gate, watching us.

"She's growing nicely," he said. He was a pleasant young man—heavy shouldered, thick, tousled, fair hair above a round face. "We've been keeping an eye on her," he went on. "We knew you'd got her."

"Oh?" I said.

"I bred her," the young man said. "I had to leave her. And the rest of them—eight pups altogether. I put them in a box in the middle of the field and rang the dogs' home. Told them where to find the pups."

"Why did you abandon them?" I said sternly.

"Had to. I was running," he said, as if it were the most obvious explanation in the world.

I was mystified. "Running?" I said.

"Yes," he said. "From the police. I had to leave everything—the van, wife, kids, everything. It's all blown over now."

"What had you done?" I asked.

"Nothing," he said, so virtuously I knew he was lying. "I hadn't done a thing."

We looked at Jess galloping about the garden, pouncing on invisible game behind the lilac trees.

"She's big," the young man said. "And fast. I'll buy her back. I'll give you a good profit, Mister."

"No, thanks," I said. "I quite like her." I started to walk toward the house when I remembered something. "Tell me," I asked, "how was she bred?"

He took a small notebook out of his pocket and turned the pages. "Here it is," he said. "I keep all the details in this book. Her father was a first-cross greyhound-deerhound. She favors him a lot—same gray color, same little whiskers. And her mother was a little brindle greyhound, very fast. I gave her to my brother after these pups were born, but she got killed up on the Downs. Ran into a fence and broke her neck. Yes, it's all down here. Born April 12th, your dog was, one of eight pups."

Gypsies call here pretty regularly, to offer me a profit. Jess would be a good dog for a travelling man. She's very fast, but it's not just her speed—she's a thinking runner. I've seen her catch seagulls on the beach, racing on the very last inch of sand next to the water so that the birds on land are unable to fly directly out to sea. They have to take off and turn back over Jess' head, and any gull that isn't above her astonishing leap is in real danger.

When I first had her, I kept her about the house for a week or two before taking her out. I put her in the back of the car one day, thinking to let her have a run near the river. When I reached the top of the village, I saw Alec Dougan come out of the post office. Alec owns a lot of land around here—a couple of thousand acres of arable land, enough pasture for a large and famous herd of Aryshires, and a stretch of woodland it takes days to cover. I stopped to talk to him.

"How are you, old son?" said Alec, eyes alight, smiling. I could see he was going to tell me the latest racy tale of local high life. And then he turned the smile off. I watched the harsh resurrection of my grandfather's dislike of lurchers come into his face—the same downturn of the lips, the same stiffening of the neck.

"What's that you've got?" he said.

"Nice, isn't she?" I said.

"You've got trouble there," he said.

"Come away, Alec," I said. "She's only a baby."

"She'll hunt," he said. "You won't be able to stop her." I could see him thinking of his pheasants. "We're old friends," he said. "I won't ask you to keep her off my land, but watch her. And don't say I didn't warn you." He went off shaking his head.

She hasn't been too hard to train, though, and she no longer hunts indiscriminately. But I have had moments of panic. Last spring, we walked on a holiday Sunday in the public woods. The paths were full of strolling groups come to see the renewed foliage of the beeches. Children ran through the grass. I had Jess on her lead, and she walked demurely at my side. Without breaking step, she dipped her long neck to a tussock, and, raising her head, gave me—put gently into my hand—a live cock pheasant. His gape wide with fright, he sat heavily on my hand. It had all been done so gracefully, so entirely without fuss, that nobody noticed at all. Completely unhurt, the bird sat there, and then, indignant, blundered off, his long tail feathers streaming.

Although I can safely whistle Jess off any chase at all now, she can still startle me. This morning the fields are covered with a light snow. It lies in the furrows and is blown in midget drifts in the lee of trees. The ground is so hard that it rings when you stamp on it. We went out early into the field behind Dr. Medlicott's house, and I slipped Jess at once. Normally she bounds immediately into a frolic, running in circles, tossing twigs in the air, but this morning her moving was quite unlike play, and I should have recognized at once that she was on to something. There is a frightening directness and velocity about her serious running, a concentration of effort that involves the whole dog, bending everything to a single purpose, that of catching and killing. Before I could purse my cold lips to a single recall, she had picked up a rabbit in the shadow of a hedge. It was a run of at least two hundred yards and the poor creature hadn't time to turn away, hadn't time to squeal before its back was snapped and Jess was bringing it back, hanging loose from her killing jaws. It's easy to understand why landowners are wary of men who walk the fields with lurchers.

It wasn't always so. Such dogs were once owned only by princes. In ancient Wales, the gift of a rough-coated greyhound was a mark of the highest royal favor, and great poets, skilled in the strict measures, wrote complex odes to their lords begging such gifts. The young hero Culhwch, journeying to Arthur's court in search of initiation and adventure, went on horseback, dressed as a prince, miraculously accoutred. His horse was a light gray, four winters old, well ribbed and shell-hoofed. His saddle was of gold, his tubular bridle bit was of gold, his battle-axe was keen enough to draw blood from the wind, his sword was hilted with gold, and his buckler was of gold and ivory. But his ultimate treasures were the two greyhounds, white-breasted, brindled, that danced and cavorted in front of him as he rode. Sufficient evidence of his nobility in themselves, they each wore a wide collar of red gold, fitting from shoulder to ear. They would have been the old, rough-coated greyhounds, exactly the lurchers I've studied for so long, since the brindle color did not exist in smooth-haired greyhounds until Lord Orford, in the eighteenth century, introduced a bulldog cross in order to improve the courage of his strain. What I am calling a lurcher is a dog that has come down unchanged through the ages; except that he was known until the seventeenth century as a greyhound, everything about him is the same. A strong, hardy dog, his lines the dominant graceful outline of the greyhound we know today, his coat longer and weather-resisting, from the occasional judicious crosses of sheepdog and deerhound, he is valued for his intelligence and ability in the field. His likeness can be seen in a thousand paintings and tapestries, because he was as necessary to the life of the court as he is now to the travelling man. Culhwch's dogs would have been true hunting dogs, bred for efficiency in all weathers, long-coated, tough. King Canute, a notably sensible man, laid down in his laws that none but a gentleman could own a greyhound, and I'm delighted by this evidence of the legitimacy of lurchers.

It wouldn't surprise me to find the lurcher becoming a fashionable dog in a year or two. It has many virtues: it is tactful, not quarrelsome; will curl up in the smallest space; is not noisy. Lurchers are big enough to be very efficient guards. I saw one walking along the Charles River in Boston two years ago, and it was evident to me that the girl who owned him was safe. It would be a desperate mugger who'd willingly face a lurcher; he'd very likely lose an arm. And they're gratifyingly good to look at; they'd cause a sensation in Greenwich Village. I saw, in a fashionable journal recently, a slim and disdainful lady, posed to display the perfection of her expensive clothes. She held on two leads two splendid lurchers. They're coming back. If I wear my country tweeds and carry an ashplant, my lurcher takes me into the most rarefied social circles; she becomes a sporting dog rather than the companion of gypsies, thieves, and tramps. Retired colonels write books about them, they are to be seen with rich racehorse owners and young men-about-town.

They are likely to be very useful very soon. As an experiment, a group of people in Wiltshire have been living for a year exactly as the ancient Celts did, raising scrubby animals, growing meager wheat, sleeping in a thatched, circular hut. They have with them two dogs—lurchers—and are loud in their praise of these animals, which have proved essential to the success of their project. Come the destruction, when the last warhead has exploded and the world is an untechnical ruin and small groups of people live desperately on what they can catch, we lurcher owners will no doubt be the new aristocrats. Because of Jess I expect I'll have a gray horse of four winters, gold all over him. I shall be a prince.

The Holm Oak

They left Southampton through Eastleigh and Chandler's Ford. The traffic was heavier than he had anticipated. A new layout, badly signposted, machines like sleeping animals at the roadside, let them bypass Winchester. Most of the trucks went north on the London road and driving was quieter on the A-34. It had rained after dawn and surfaces were steaming in the early sun. Just before Newbury, near Beacon Hill, they stopped for a flask of coffee. Humps of small tumuli, round and smooth, stood nearby in the ancient fields. They disturbed Rhodri. He was not of their time, nor of their place. The bones in those old graves were alien to him. The gentle country, almost treeless, brought him no warmth. Elizabeth sat in the car, relaxed, smiling so faintly that he alone could know it. He drove on towards the M-4.

He took the slope to the motorway and his wife, turning to the rear window, told him all was clear.

"Not a thing in sight," Elizabeth said. "Not a thing."

She was suddenly alert, consciously enjoying the journey. He sidled the car across the empty road into the fast lane, slick as oil through the gears, accelerating.

"Not bad," Elizabeth said. "That's the best bit of driving you've done today."

"I know," he said. "I did it from memory. I used to climb that ramp every Friday night when my father was ill, so my hands just took over."

Ahead of them, appearing and reappearing among the undulations of the road, files of small cars, five or six at a time, keeping together as if for protection, scurried westwards.

"Every Friday I did it," Rhodri said, "for over three years. One summer I drove the Alfa Romeo. What a car. Sammy told me when I bought it I should have bought a mechanic to go with it. It never let me down on this journey, otherwise it was utterly hopeless. British racing green, it was. I used to come down this road, ninety, ninety-five, roaring like a lion."

"What happened to it?" said Elizabeth. She'd heard it before. She liked him to talk when he was driving.

"I gave it to a fellow in the math department," Rhodri said, "Gary Lewis, bright lad, good with cars. I'd had enough. It blew up in Portland Terrace and I pushed it into a side street. I never saw it again. This car's a bit different, though. This is luxury. Good of Sara to lend it."

"She'd lend you her arms and legs," Elizabeth said. "She thinks you're perfect."

Rhodri saw his sister, nine years old again, her long, thin legs, her hair rioting, her angular, frightening energy. Every day she had taken him to school, fierce and protective, his hand grasped in her hard hand. The day he had fallen out of an apple tree in Thomas' orchard, she had lifted him into the old man's wheelbarrow and pushed him all the way home, both of them bawling. Once she had stood between Rhodri and the headmaster, when the man had threatened punishment. She had stood there tensely, not moving, full of quiet fury. Griffiths, the man's name had been, Mr. Griffiths, a tall, fair man. He had turned away, helpless against her, amused and chagrined. Sara had been thirteen then.

Fine rain began to fall as they crossed the Severn Bridge, but the roads were drying and the washed fields green and fresh when they left the motorway near Chepstow and travelled quiet ways to Usk. The northern slopes of the Beacons were already shadowed with purple, the river, silver under a reflected sky, ran on benignly.

"It looks lovely, doesn't it," Rhodri said, "the great, comfortable flanks of Mother Earth, the green valley below them. But in winter those hills are killers. Remember Margaret Harris?"

"No," said Elizabeth, "before my time probably."

"I didn't know her," Rhodri said. "Her brother Aled was at the university with me. She was a district nurse in these parts, visited the sick in their homes, mothers with new babies, that sort of thing. She went out one winter morning to one of the hill farms, the snow came, blotted everything out. They found her a few yards from her car, frozen to death. It's not only the cold, it's the wind that goes with it."

Below them, at the river's edge, two anglers, unmoving as heron, watched their lines float down the lazy stream.

A neighbor had lit a fire in the grate when they reached the old house, but it had done nothing to disperse the heavy smell of damp which filled the rooms. An uncomfortable chill soon depressed Rhodri. But for a few weeks in August, the house was rarely used. Elizabeth threw open the doors, pulled down the windows. A thin blue film of neglect covered the floors, the sills, the arms and backs of chairs. After their father's death Sara had taken the best of the furniture, the round dining table and its eight chairs, the Georgian corner cupboard, good Swansea china which had belonged to their great-grandmother, the long-case clock which showed not only the time, but the phases of the moon. Sara had all these. They shone in her immaculate house in Southampton, under her guardian eye. What was left was workaday stuff, familiar to Rhodri as the skin of his hands. The big pine table, its top scrubbed white in his mother's day, was gray now. Inexplicable stains were sunk deep in the soft wood. They had eaten at this table. He had run home from school knowing that it would be covered with the great meals of his mother's kitchen, loaves straight from the oven, salt bacon, pies and cakes. Afterwards, all cleared away, it was there he sat doing his homework, the house quiet and warm, an oil lamp hanging in a shaped metal bracket from the ceiling, another, the liquid visible in the ruby glass of its bowl, behind his books. Electricity had been late arriving at the farm. His father would have been reading in his wooden armchair, awkwardly at one side so that his dog

Cymro, one-eyed, testy and much loved, could sit with him. Now the chair stood in its dust against the wall. It was a dead house.

Outside the air was warm and very still. Several farms away a dog barked, without anger. The brown remains of February snowdrops lay withered in the grass opposite the front door. Rhodri leaned on the gate into the top field. The land fell away in a gentle slope and the far hedge was hidden, but for the big oak. His father had loved the one tree. It was an evergreen oak, a holm oak, the only one, they had believed, in the county. The last of the sunlight was falling on its glossy leaves.

Once, a small boy, he had found his father standing under the tree. He had climbed through the fields from the river and his father was standing in the deep shade of the tree. He was completely still, his head bowed, his outstretched hand just touching the tree's bark. His eyes, Rhodri had seen, were open. There was about the man's stillness an absence which had frightened the little boy. Rhodri had gone home troubled, and now the memory, coming to him unasked, made him fretful and anxious. He lifted the cases from the car and carried them indoors.

"The beds are fine," Elizabeth said, "Mrs. Evans has kept them beautifully aired. We shan't catch pneumonia."

She looked about her, assessing what was to be done before she would think the house warm and comfortable. A little elbow grease, she thought, a little paint. It could be worse.

"Come and have your supper," she said.

The morning, perfect as memory, brought its peace to Rhodri. Together, he and Elizabeth restored the house to order, swept the floors, began to clean the windows. The late spring air, mild and clear, invaded the rooms and passages, refreshed them. When, after lunch, Phil Rees stopped his Land Rover in the yard, Rhodri went cheerfully to meet him. Phil had been in the same class in the village school. They had known each other for over thirty years. Once, when they were eight or nine, they had been two of a group of children wildly excited because school had just ended for the summer holidays. They had marched, singing and laughing and waving sticks pulled from the hedge, along the road, down the lane past the farm, down the hill and up the other side, exulting, not stopping until they returned to the village. For Rhodri, a shy boy, almost without friends, it had been a vision. It had seemed to him then that he had never seen such colors, heard such voices, known such excitement. Phil Rees had worn a jersey of so clear a blue that Rhodri knew he would never see its like again. But now Phil was a heavy man, round-shouldered, shrewd. He climbed out of the Land Rover.

"Welcome home, Rhodri," he said. "How long are you down for?" He walked to the field gate and leaned his arms on the top spar, his movements slow, deliberate.

"Your grass looks good," he said. "Young Mervyn keeps the grass very well for you."

Together they looked across the grass, vivid and weedless.

"There used to be wild orchids in this field in my father's day," Rhodri said.

"Selective weedkillers nowadays," Phil said. "They keep the grass wonderfully clean. And let's face it, your Dad didn't mind a few odd weeds on his land."

Rhodri smiled. It was true. His father had kept his pastures untouched, but for a little fertilizer. He had loved the purple orchises, old inhabitants of the fields.

"Not the best of farmers," said Rhodri, "but we miss him. He's been dead—seven years, is it?—and we all miss him."

"Remember the time he tried to start a herd of Jerseys?" said Phil. "Jerseys, up here? He had no chance."

"He liked quality," Rhodri said. "He couldn't stand an animal without a touch of class."

"Well, we miss him," Phil said. "He was the brightest man for miles around, always reading. He knew about music and medicine. When I was a kid he taught me the names of the stars. He was the man we went to when there was trouble."

"He was a fine man," Rhodri said.

"Like a lawyer," Phil said. "We need him now, with all these EEC rules for milk farmers. He would have filled the forms in for us, gone down to Carmarthen to represent us. We've been sadly helpless since he's gone."

Rhodri nodded at his old friend. He knew how involved his father had been in the small community.

"Oh, we all depended on him," Phil said. "He could talk to anyone. He would just put his old hat on his head, and he was as good as any man. He was an aristocrat."

"There must be someone else," Rhodri said.

"Not like your father," Phil said quickly. "Your Sara could have done it, but she had to go off to be a doctor. And you, you look like your father, you're tall and slow-moving and like him in the face, but you never cared for the place. You were always going to be a stranger."

"That's not true, Phil," Rhodri said. He was more deeply hurt than he had imagined possible.

"Look at you," said Phil, "in your expensive clothes, your shirt, your soft pullover, your American shoes. You don't begin to look as if you belong here."

"You resent me," said Rhodri, "by God, Phil, you resent me coming back."

"I'm sorry," said Phil, "I shouldn't have said that. You have to go where your work is, I suppose. But I pass this house four times every day and I see its blind windows and I think of the cobwebs building up inside. There aren't any voices, not of people or animals. It isn't right. There you are in America and the house is falling down. The rain only has to get in under the slates and it's finished. Why don't you sell it?"

"It's been our house for more than three hundred years," Rhodri said, "I couldn't."

"It's useless as it is," said Phil. "A young man could make a good living in it. Think of a strong youngster now, with his wife and a child or two, what he could do with this place. The land's in good heart, let it go."

Rhodri, conscious of anger, did not answer.

"Seven years ago," Phil said, "I saw your father by that old oak of his. I'd have had it down years ago, if it had been mine. He was looking very rough, yellow in the face, moving slow and painful. What's up, Mr. Llewellyn, I said. He told me then he was dying, that he had cancer. He knew all about it. We stood there in the field and we talked, man to man."

"I know that," Rhodri said. "I've always been jealous of that. To talk to him as you did and under those circumstances was my right. I am his son."

"That day I was his son," Phil said. "A man can be another man's son, and in his turn he can be another man's father, when the need is there. You were in New York, and I was here."

Elizabeth sat in her clean house. She could do no more until they decided what was to be redecorated. The floors gleamed, the cupboards were neat, everything was in its place.

"I see Phil's in good voice," she said.

"You didn't come out," Rhodri said, "he would have liked to speak to you."

"I thought you were involved in some serious talking," Elizabeth said, "your face was black as thunder."

"He wants me to sell the farm," Rhodri said.

"What did he say?" Elizabeth said. Her voice was tranquil, very neutral.

"This has always been our place," Rhodri said, "he knows that."

He sat in his father's chair, his legs stretched before him, trying consciously to relax, to appear as if he were not upset.

"He seemed to think that I have a duty to the community to make sure someone lived here," he said querulously.

"He has a point," Elizabeth said. "We can't use the place, we don't need it. Once we get back to New York we never think of it."

"I don't have to think of it," Rhodri said. "I know it's here, always."

"Oh, come away," Elizabeth said, "I've seen you. You can't wait to get back to your laboratory."

The fire was burning freely and generously, the last of the old apple wood, cut years ago and stored in the shed. When evening came it would dance away the shadows in the corners of the room, it would easily keep away the cold which would come as the sun went down.

"Phil had a good word for my father," said Rhodri. "Blamed me for not being as good a man."

"He was remarkable," Elizabeth said. "So handsome, so tolerant. I found some of his old diaries in the dresser drawer and I've been reading them. He was brilliantly able. He was wasted here."

"That's not what Phil thinks," Rhodri said, "he thinks they need someone like him, they still miss him."

"I don't doubt it," Elizabeth said, "but you've read those yearbooks of his. Oh, how tragic, that evidence of an intelligence searching without guidance, his vast chaotic reading, his amazing information. His insights were often splendid, and often hopelessly wrong. Imagine what he could have done, given an education."

"I know," Rhodri said. "For years he was convinced that the world was six thousand years old, then he discovered archaeology. And there he was, into carbon dating and all the rest of it. He used to stay up into the early hours reading my math books."

"He wasn't going to have you like that," Elizabeth said.

"No," said Rhodri. "He pointed me at a university the day I started school, and Sara before me."

"He was wise as well as clever," Elizabeth said. "He was locked into this place. He was going to make sure you were free. How delighted he would be to know of the concerts and plays you go to, that you've heard all the great tenors, seen Olivier and Guinness."

"Olivier was his idol," Rhodri said. "When I saw him in *Othello* years ago I sent my father a full account, theatre program, everything. He kept all my letters. I suppose they're still here, somewhere."

"Sara has them," Elizabeth said. "She has this foolish idea that one day you'll be a great man and she can edit a collection of your letters."

Rhodri smiled, leaned back, looked thoughtfully at his long hands as they lay idle on the arms of the chair.

"I'd have to offer it to Mervyn first," he said, "if ever I sold this place. He might not want the house though, he's not married."

"He's only twenty-four, give him time," Elizabeth said. "It's not a bad idea. He's kept the fields well for so young a man. And he is your cousin, it isn't as if it were going right away."

"His mother was my mother's cousin," Rhodri said. "He's not a Llewellyn."

142

"What's it matter?" Elizabeth said, with sudden passion. "Can't you see your father wanted away from this place, made sure his children got away? What is there for you here? Sell it, rent it, give it away, we don't need the money. Forty-six acres of thin topsoil on a hill. If someone needs it, can live on it, can start three centuries of a family on it, let them have it. We, you and I, are at the end of the line, transient. The land will always be here, but we shan't."

Rhodri stood abruptly, grinning down at his wife, her flushed and ardent face.

"What are you going to do?" she asked.

He shrugged his shoulders, pulled down the corners of his rueful mouth. "I don't know," he said.

He went out into the field and looked west. The holm oak was dark against the end of the sun. He walked towards it and looked at it carefully. He knew it from its topmost leaf to the grass about its base. There, he said, is the snag on which I used to climb into its branches, there the limb to which Sara climbed to tie a rope. She had fastened an old tire to the rope and it had been their swing for years. He walked about the tree, noting it. It was an act of something more than mere recognition; he knew the tree. He knew every inch of its bark, the shape and substance of its regenerating head, the quality of its dead leaves as they fell to the grass, the sturdy thrust of its trunk, the noise it made in storms. He knew that it grew within him with the same accuracy and certainty and stubborn reality, that he was aware of the great claws of its roots, grasping the land he had always thought his own.

He closed his eyes. The tree was still with him. He could not imagine any power strong enough to uproot it.

Reverse for
Dennis

Once a year, on the first day of March, on St. David's Day, we held in our school an *eisteddfod,* a celebration and performance of those arts and that culture for which the Welsh are held to be preeminent. It was quite popular with the boys. Preparations for the event disrupted the orderly procedure of the school throughout the dark month of February, and a clever boy, entering a shrewd selection of events, could wander at will about the damp corridors for weeks on end, pretending here that he was on his way to recite Kipling's "If" to an eager committee of listeners in the library, and claiming there that he was going to collect his sheaf of watercolors, a late entry for the fine art section. Above all, the ebullient competitive spirit which lay uneasily dormant within us was stimulated into constructive action. Serious boys could be heard muttering aloud the sculptured periods of their speeches, learned boys searched the pages of the *Shorter Oxford English Dictionary* for words absurd and recondite enough to cause gasps of amazement on the day. Some of us gave up, temporarily, our more normal activities, fighting, football, the cunning evasion of all serious and responsible behavior.

I was quite good at the *eisteddfod* business, if for an unlikely reason. Unwilling to expose myself to the good-humored public banter of my fellows, I did not enter the singing competitions, or the verse speaking, or even the impromptu speech, the real motivation of which was the subtle introduction of as many double-entendres as possible.

The best speakers never reached the finals of this event. My friend Arthur Purcell, whose grandfather was a local politician noted for polysyllabic eloquence, was marvelous at the impromptu speech. Only Michael Cleary could equal him. Their wild, irreverent humor, their wayward scorn, their biting awareness of every weakness of the ruling dynasty of our establishment, ensured their regular abrupt dismissal from the competition.

Michael Cleary left school early, running away to work in a racing stable where he soon became a steeplechase jockey. Occasionally he would send us photographs of himself being spectacularly separated from a horse as it collapsed in mid-air above some disastrous fence or other. He was a great loss to us all. But Arthur Purcell remained, the sharp barbs of his wit growing more bitter and outrageous. Nobody was immune from his sudden, puncturing sallies.

It was in the written competitions that I made my territory. These were entered anonymously, our identities hidden by noms de plume. I excelled in the manufacture of such aliases, loved the discovery of the many masks I used. It is true that my enthusiasm meant that I had to write essay upon essay, poem after poem, in order to employ the names I invented, but I would not abandon them.

So the Tutankhaman Kid would provide a hurried ode on the mutability of the seasons, Boudoir of Splendid Petals a superficial defense of belligerence as an art, K. Ataturk III some wry platitudes about the necessity of civilization.

Once, by error, I won the essay prize for fifteen-year-olds. The judge, a retired man of letters, unsmiling, dry in every joint, announced the negative qualities which had induced him—in an admittedly bad year—to award me first place. "First then," he had said, holding my pages at arm's length, between thumb and finger, "first is 'Oblomov Rides Again.' Whoever he may be." I stood up with a casual modesty designed to deceive nobody and acknowledged my identity. "A great thing, but

146

mine own," said Arthur Purcell, kicking me on the ankle with just enough force to enable me to hold back a cry of pain. And all about me my friends mimed horrified and exaggerated surprise.

The next year, as Felis Concolor Couguar, a character I had discovered in a life of John James Audubon, I won the poetry competition with some energetic lines about a cat. This was my greatest triumph. In fact, Couguar's poem was not at all bad. He had modified it with some skill from a poem by D. H. Lawrence.

The literary events were always decided in the morning of St. David's Day; musical competitions took place during the afternoon and evening. We sat, the afternoon of Couguar's victory, listening to choir upon choir, to solo violins, to oboes, flutes and harps, to the smirking vocalists. I remember none of them. Late in the day, when we could see only the darkness of evening through the high windows, and dim lights hung from the beams above us, a young man got up to announce the results of the musical composition. Our composers had been asked to set, for voice and piano accompaniment, "To Daffodils," by Robert Herrick.

Arthur Purcell and I had read this poem and we preferred not to think of it. In our opinion, to set it to music was an occupation for idiots. But one competitor, said the young man, had done it brilliantly. His nom de plume, he announced, was *Sinned*. A connoisseur of such disguises, I was stunned by the implications of this one, by its brevity, by the force and subtlety of its attack. I sat up. Who could it be?

"I think," said the headmaster briskly, "we can guess who this is. It's Dennis Williams, isn't it. He's written his name backwards."

I recognized this as an act of genius. He had transformed his mild, placatory, given name, the name of a saint, into a monosyllable of unseemly power.

I had seen Dennis Williams many times before, but had never really looked at him. He stood, tall and slender, perhaps a year older than I was. His smooth pale face was closed and tranquil, he was smiling very gently to himself. He wore a coat of speckled Irish tweed and gray worsted trousers, beautifully cut, very expensive. His hair, thick and wavy and parted on the left, was a vivid and truculent red.

"A contemporary sensibility," said the judge. "An exciting talent, a gift for the unexpected phrase." Dennis Williams gazed thoughtfully at some spot on the far wall. Asked to go to the piano to play the accompaniment, he shrugged slightly and walked through the rows of seated boys as if he did not see them. He carried always with him his own agreeable solitude.

His soloist was Idwal Rowlands, a hulking boy whose voice remained, despite his fifteen years, a pure and flawless soprano. He was six feet tall, and solid. His face was a choirboy's face, round, pink and sincere, and comically irrelevant above his brawny frame. Beside me Arthur Purcell, struck afresh by the incongruity of that ill-matched voice and body, shook with stifled laughing. I looked at Dennis Williams as he began to play. He struck from the keys a handful of jeering chords and a tinkle of dissonance. Idwal Rowlands wrinkled his clear brow and prepared to sing. "Fair daffodils," he piped, "we weep to see You haste away so soon; / As yet the early-rising sun Has not attain'd his noon." All about me, affected by Arthur's snorted giggles, boys were staring glassy-eyed and rosy in their efforts not to laugh. Spike Hughes had stuffed his handkerchief into his mouth. "Stay, stay until the hasting day," carolled enormous Idwal, oblivious of us all.

Then suddenly we became aware, nearly all of us, of the piano. Alongside the dulcet melody, almost a parody of the sweet noise of the words, Dennis Williams was playing a sharp and mocking accompaniment, pointed, jagged, telling us something of a sturdy despair at once profound and full of energy. It was an astonishing experience. Our applause was puzzled, respectful. Afterwards I went up to Dennis and told him how much I had liked the song. He gave the faintest indication of a smile, said nothing.

I would like to claim that Dennis Williams had been my friend, but it would not be true. Quiet, amiable, impregnably self-sufficient, he seemed alone even when with other boys. He moved, tall and relaxed, on the edges of my life, where we nodded to each other. Once I saw him rowing, alone, on the lake at the edge of the school grounds, and I waved to him.

He brought in his heavy boat, spinning the oars expertly, and invited me to join him.

As I stepped into the boat I saw his large, nimble hands, the thickness of his long wrists. We didn't say much, just moved without effort over the simple water, above the weeds, above the still trout. That was a perfect afternoon, one preserved against time. And once, walking through the small park behind Wesley Street, I came upon Dennis sitting on a bench, his long legs stretched before him, his eyes almost shut against his cool knowledge. He was eighteen then. I thought him cultivated and experienced far beyond my achievement.

That evening my cousin Sara met me in High Street.

"I didn't know," she said, "that you were a friend of Dennis Williams." It was almost an accusation.

"I'm not," I said.

"Don't be silly," she said, "I saw you in the park this afternoon. Talking together, the pair of you, thick as thieves." The world to her was uncomplicated and direct, she sparkled with energy.

"Maybe," I said, "but we aren't friends. We just talk to each other sometimes." I looked at her doubtfully. It was the sort of inane statement she would not accept. But she was gazing past me with a look of ethereal greed.

"He's lovely," she said. "Dreamy." I was appalled. Such behavior was frighteningly untypical of Sara.

"You're mad," I said. She didn't answer.

"Dreamy!" I sneered.

"So handsome," Sara said.

I thought about it for a while and could not agree. I objected. "His hair is red," I said.

"What's that got to do with it, fool," said Sara, and she turned away to walk up the road with bustling, confident steps.

Well, Dennis Williams had a lot of class, I recognized that. His father was a doctor, rich and popular. Dennis always dressed beautifully, he took long holidays abroad, he was generous and softspoken. I could see what Sara meant. In September he was going to medical school. I saw him, late in August, walking over the golf course with his Airedale, Max. He had an old walking stick which he threw for the dog to retrieve.

I've always liked Airedales and Max was a good one. No longer young, gray was beginning to fleck the black of his saddle, but he still ran like a puppy after that stick. Dennis took it from the dog and waited at the edge of a bunker for me to come up to them.

He told me then that he was going to Edinburgh to study medicine.

"My father went there," he said. "I've always wanted to be a doctor."

It was a hot evening. The course was deserted but for three figures on a distant green. We could hear them laughing.

"That's great, Dennis," I said. I bent down to pat the old dog. "What about your music?" I said. "I thought you were keen on music." Dennis was scratching his initials into the sandy turf with the ferrule of his stick, faintly, patiently, with infinite care, so that I could scarcely see the letters.

"Music?" he said. "That's just playing about, isn't it!" And then, with a sudden irritation he ripped through the impeccable *D* and *W* until the scored grass held no trace of them.

I don't know what went wrong at Edinburgh. I was busy with my own affairs, growing older, learning to be cool and fashionable, to be amused at everything. But in the spring and early summer of the next year I began to see Dennis about, and someone told me that he was no longer going to be a doctor, that he had given up medical school and was working in a lawyer's office. I knew the place. My friend, Willie John Edwards, was a junior clerk there. Whenever I saw him, Dennis looked all right; I mean he looked happy, in control. We didn't say much to each other.

I asked Willie John about Dennis.

"He's strange," Willie John said. "He's so quiet. He'll be in the office an hour before you know he's there. Doesn't talk, doesn't whistle. If you make a joke, he just smiles. He's a nice, strange fellow."

"He's always been like that," I said.

"He's bright," Willie John told me. "He's very bright. He'll make a good lawyer, everybody says so."

It was just a casual conversation I had with Willie John one day when we were playing tennis. Frankly, I didn't think about Dennis very often.

But it was a shock when I learned he was dead. That August, in the year I was eighteen, I went to London for a fortnight, to stay with my aunt in Dulwich Village. I was going to the university that next term. I took to London, had a great time, saw all the galleries, most of the theatres, two famous athletics meetings at The White City. I was reluctant to go home. The day I travelled back was wickedly hot. I hung about in Cardiff waiting for a train to carry me through the narrowing valleys and everything was dry, powdered with dust. Children sat in whatever little pools of shade they could find, and the city drowsed. I reached the last station in late afternoon and humped my bag into the yard. There was no taxi and I walked two miles to the house, uphill all the way. I think of that walk with surprise now, but it was nothing to me then. I could have walked twenty miles without fatigue. There was no one at home. I made myself a meal, took a shower, went out into the lengthening evening.

Downtown I saw Harry Pritchard, a boy I'd known for years. Harry was very surprising; in less than twelve months he'd grown from one of the smallest boys around into a thin giant of six feet three inches. He'd not long joined the police force.

"Coming to the cinema?" he said. "It's cool, and there's a smashing double feature—*The Mummy* and *The Return of Frankenstein*.

"Oh Harry," I said, "your appetite for the Gothic is voracious and unsubtle."

"Sticks and stones," he said contentedly. "Come on, I'll buy you an ice cream."

The cinema was almost empty. It was pleasant there in the cool gloom.

"What about your friend, then?" Harry said. "What about poor Dennis Williams?"

"What about him?" I said. I was thinking of the colossal technique of an American hurdler I'd seen at The White City. He'd risen like a bird to every obstacle, his stride unchecked, his rhythm smooth and effortless. He had won by a distance.

"Come on," Harry said, "don't pretend you haven't heard."

151

"I've been up in London," I said. "Didn't get back until six o'clock. Tell me all."

"He's dead," Harry said. "Dead and buried. He gassed himself over a week ago, nearly a fortnight ago. Silly little fool, no need for it."

I sat there, looking at the frivolous horror on the screen. "Why did he do it?" I said.

"Absolutely no need," said Harry roughly. I could hear the indignation in his voice.

"Some girl," he said, "told him she was pregnant and he was responsible. You'd think he'd have gone along to somebody, for help, for advice. We don't live in the Dark Ages, for God's sake."

"Dennis wouldn't go to anybody," I said. "He was always his own man, he'd come to his own decisions. He always seemed to me to be sufficient to himself."

"He was a fool, then," said Harry. "How did he know the girl was telling the truth? She could have been mistaken. Why didn't he go to his father? His father's a doctor, he'd know what to do."

I didn't answer. I was helpless in the dark of the cinema, unable to understand. "He had a lot of style," I said at last, "Dennis would have done it with style. It would have been a superb gesture." I didn't mean anything. It was an attempt to claim for Dennis his individuality, his singular quality, a defense in my mind against the tragedy of his action.

But it made Harry angry. He leaned over and began to mutter vehemently to me. "Style, is it!" he said, very quietly and quickly. "Style?—it was a hideous and ugly suicide, that's what it was. Do you know who found him? Willie John Edwards found him. Willie John, without an ounce of harm in him. There's not much style about that." He sat back, outraged.

"Oh," I said, surprised, "it happened in the office."

"Yes," said Harry, "he went in on the Sunday evening, late, and he wasn't found until Willie John opened the doors on Monday morning."

"Poor old boy," I said, pitying both of them.

"He was in a terrible mess," Harry Pritchard said. "Terrible. They go an inhuman color, did you know that?"

"No," I said. I could see Dennis Williams playing "To Daffodils," hear Idwal Rowlands' sad, high voice. It seemed a long time ago. "And his hair," Harry Pritchard said. "That lovely red hair of his. It had turned quite dark. When they carried him out I saw his hair had turned dark."

Then I knew that Dennis Williams was indeed dead, that he had gone from the world forever. It was the detail of the hair that got me. We sat in the electronic darkness for a long time, silent, unmoving. "Oh hell," Harry said, "this is a miserable old world. Why don't we go out into the daylight and look at it?" We walked out and the sun still shone. Two little boys, perhaps ten or eleven years old, passed us, laughing, their arms brown as summer.

A Piece of
Archangel

Oscar came over on Saturday morning and we measured the room for the bookshelves I wanted. I made a rough drawing of the sort of thing I imagined, we decided on the lengths of cut timber we'd need, and Oscar made a list of them. I got ready to go down to the sawmills.

"What shall I get, Oscar," I asked, "deal or pine?"

"Get what you can as long as it's straight," Oscar said. "Wood is like gold these days."

We've done a lot of jobs together in this house, so many that I'm accepted at the sawmills as a genuine self-employed carpenter, able to buy my timber at trade rates; but I always dress the part, wear overalls, push a steel rule in my pocket. I saunter into the office with bravado. Oscar, the genuine tradesman, laughs at my act.

"You'd better get parana pine," he said. "It's reliable, and cheaper than deal. Some of it is pretty."

I took the wagon through the town and stopped on the river bridge before I reached the wharves. The tide was on the turn and the river was momentarily without turbulence, holding a brief calm between the weight of the incoming sea and its own heavy direction down the valley. The sea trout were in. I could see them lying in irregular columns, heads upstream, unmoving. They'd run with the tide, though, once it turned. Thinking of fishing, I drove on toward the river wharf, to the sawmills. Two old men were hauling planks from a rack of hardwood close by. I stopped near the office and walked in through the trade entrance. Gus wasn't there. There was a brass bell on the counter, an old one with a plunger on top. When you smack the plunger with the flat of your hand some kind of striking mechanism is activated. I gave it a try, knowing that all I'd hear would be an unmetallic thud. It never worked. It was probably the oldest bell of its kind in the south of England. The whole office was a museum. On its walls were advertisements for products which had been unobtainable for thirty years or more, samples of ancient and outmoded remedies for damp walls and leaking roofs stood on the shelves. Gus wouldn't have a thing changed in his office. I settled down to wait.

I'd been there about five minutes, leaning on the counter, dreaming, when the door opened and a young man came in. His name is Hardisty and he's a jobbing builder in the neighborhood, can turn his hand to anything. We're on nodding terms. He's thin and fair and perhaps twenty-five years old.

"Gus not in then?" he said.

"When is Gus ever in," I answered.

"Lazy old basket," he said. "Gone off to have a cup of tea, I shouldn't wonder."

He took out a cigarette and began to sing softly to himself. We waited in amiable patience until Gus arrived, bustling.

"Right, sirs and gents," he said. "Who's first?"

Gus is a little, wiry man, with a crest of white hair. He looks and moves like a terrier, all eagerness and swift little legs. I pushed my list towards him. He read it slowly, pursing his lips, shaking his head doubtfully.

"Oh, come on, Gus," I said. "There's nothing difficult there."

"I don't know, I don't know," said Gus. "There's this six-by-one, we might not have this six-by-one. Want it prepared, do you?"

He looked up as the old man came in, closing the door slowly behind him.

"Here they come," Gus said. "We've got all the rogues in this morning. Hullo, Ted."

"Prepared, Gus," I said. "Prepared and cut to those sizes."

"Oh dear, oh dear," he said, "and Saturday morning too. You know the boys will want to leave early. It's half-day, you know that."

"Stop moaning, Gus," said the old man. "Get on with it and give the man his wood."

"You want it in parana pine?" Gus said. "What's it for, shelves?"

"Yes," I said, "I'll want it nice and square."

Gus shot through the door.

"You'll be lucky," the old man said. "There's no square timber these days. They don't season it, they send it out green. Damned if it wouldn't grow if you stuck it in the ground."

Hardisty and I nodded. The old man slid down and squatted against the wall, prepared for a long wait.

"I know where there is some good stuff," the old man said, "marvelous stuff. Down in Marlborough Square. They're breaking up those big old houses, what material! The floor boards are eighteen inches wide and never a shake in them. I can't think why they're pulling those houses down, marvelous boards, they are. You'd have to get all the old polish off, all the varnish, sand them down to the clean wood. But you'd have something when you finished. All oak it is. You'd have the heart of England there."

"They got any doors there?" Hardisty asked. "I could just do with a couple of good doors."

"Doors?" said the old man. "I should think they have. Why, those doors are the real thing, beautiful solid panels, made true all those years ago by fine craftsmen out of honest wood, not this stuff they send out today. And lovely fanlights over them, not Georgian, no, Victorian. Of course, it just depends on how they were taken out. If they've been ripped out by the monkeys they employ today, well, you'll have to look at the hinges. Solid brass, those hinges, solid brass hinges, big, smooth. Swing like a Rolls-Royce they do. It makes me boil to think of those hinges being ripped out, those lovely screws driven into the wood, straight and true, countersunk perfectly, all those years ago. My old man worked in Marlborough Square, when they were building. Before I was born, that was. Have they got doors? It would take the three of us to carry one of them!"

"Thanks, Ted," said Hardisty. "I could just do with a couple of good doors. I might go down and have a look at them later on."

He looked out of the window across the river. The wind was whipping the surface of the river and a few hunched gulls sat on the mooring-posts.

"It doesn't get any warmer, does it," he said. "Here it is, nearly September and we've had no summer."

"I'm retired," said the old man. "I been retired seven years. Seventy-two I am. I can pick and choose my jobs. I only do what I fancy, a bit of cabinetmaking, a bit of quality repairing."

"You're lucky, then," said Hardisty.

"I am, that," old Ted said. "I wouldn't like to work with the muck they sell you today, especially on the building. I don't have anything to do with the building now. Carpentry? They don't know what it is. Anybody with a hammer and a couple of six-inch nails is a carpenter these days."

We said nothing for a long minute.

"Here," said the old man. "This will surprise you. Do you know what I found in my shed the other day? I went down for a bit of timber—I always keep a tidy little stock, keep it nice and dry, stack it properly with air circulating all round it—I went down there for a bit of timber and, right at the back, what do you think I found? I found a piece of archangel."

I looked at Hardisty for help, but he turned up his palms and lifted his eyebrows in mimic ignorance.

"Forgotten I had it there," said Ted, immensely satisfied. "I put it away again. 'That'll come for something special,' I said to myself. Nice little piece of ten-by-one it is, about nine foot long."

"I can't think," I said cautiously, "when I last saw a piece of archangel."

"I haven't seen any since the War," Ted said. "Oh, I saw plenty during the War. I don't suppose this boy has ever seen any."

"I haven't," said Hardisty. "I don't know what you're talking about. What is archangel, anyway?"

"There," said Ted, "I knew he hadn't seen any. Timber, that's what archangel was. Long planks of beautiful white

158

timber. Softwood, it was. Came out of Russia, from a forest near Archangel. That's how it got its name. It used to come into Littlehampton and Shoreham on Russian boats, great lengths of it, with the grain running on and on, straight as a ruler. Never a knot in sight. It was lovely.''

"Expensive, was it?'' Hardisty asked.

"No, it was cheap,'' Ted said. "It was quite cheap. And what wood to work! It would cut like cheese and wear forever. You could polish it with your handkerchief. I used to love working with it. We used it everywhere. I'd put in a floor of archangel, every plank snug and tight, all running smooth from wall to wall, and I'd look at it. It was so white I didn't like to walk on it, I didn't like to leave the marks of my boots on it. White as snow. Or silver, more like. That's it, silver.''

"Where is it now, Ted?'' I asked.

"Gone,'' he said. "All of it gone. The Russians used it all up in the war, most like.''

"They've got other forests, I bet,'' Hardisty said. "They just don't want us to have the stuff.''

"No,'' said Ted. "It's all gone. Once you start to cut down trees it doesn't take long. When I was young you could buy English oak, beech, what you liked. Not now. All over the world the great forests are going. You'd think they would never end, but they do. And we're so spendthrift, so extravagant. We use the best wood first. The best always goes first.''

Gus rushed into the office and drew his order book towards him, tucking the thin blue carbon paper under the top sheet.

"You're lucky,'' he said. "We found you some nice stuff, some really pretty pine. It'll work up nicely. Shelves, you said?''

"Bookshelves,'' I said, "thanks, Gus.''

He wrote out my ticket laboriously. He's short of two fingers on his right hand, lost them in the sawmills when he was a boy, and since then he's worked in the trade office, over thirty years. He still finds writing hard. He's nice enough, is Gus. I paid him, and went outside to load my timber into the wagon. Hardisty was busy explaining his needs to Gus and I said goodbye to old Ted. The wood was ready in a neat pile right by my wagon. I loaded it and drove away.

Oscar was sitting in the sun when I got back. He'd set up his portable bench and all his tools were ready, his chisels and screwdrivers, his electric saw, his sander. We took the sawn wood out of the wagon and looked at it carefully, piece by piece.

"It's not bad," Oscar said. "The long pieces are all slightly out of true, but by the time we screw them into place they'll be all right."

We worked quietly together, measuring, sanding, setting the frame square. The shelves began to take on the tall, spare shape I'd hoped for. At lunch time we sat together on the patio, eating sandwiches. I ran my hand along the smooth length of one of the planks. The grain was lovely, a faint pink running through it.

"It looks good," I said to Oscar.

"It'll make up pretty well," Oscar said, looking calmly down at the shelves. "We'll put a couple of right-angle brackets on the corners, at the back where you won't see them. It'll be firm enough then."

"You ever see any archangel, Oscar?" I said.

He looked at me, grinning.

"Wherever did you hear of that?" he said. It isn't often I surprise Oscar. I told him about the old man at the sawmills.

"That'll be old Ted Armitage," Oscar said, "I know old Ted. He used to work with my grandfather from time to time. Ted would know about archangel, all right."

"You ever see any?" I said.

"Of course," he said. "I used to follow my grandfather all over the place when I was a kid. I lived in his workshop, worked harder there than I ever did at school. He kept all sorts of timber in his little yard. He had a lot of rosewood one time—he loved hardwood, did my grandfather. He taught me pretty well everything I know. He told me all about archangel."

"I didn't know about your grandfather," I said.

"How could you?" Oscar said. "You've not lived here above ten years. My grandfather was dead when you came to this house. Well known and respected he was in these parts. He left me all his tools, his lovely chisels, thin and glittering, his saws, his huge square old planes, smoothing planes and jack planes. Over a hundred years old they are, beautiful. I've still got them. Nobody will ever use them again, not with the power tools we have nowadays. My old lad would have spurned this job we're doing today.''

He looked mildly down at our making bookshelves. I'd known Oscar since I first came to this house and called him in to put up a flight of stairs into the loft. He was young then, in his late twenties, quick moving and impulsive. He's settled a lot, but he still has his easy confidence, the assurance brought to him by his precise skills.

''What's wrong with it?'' I said. ''What's wrong with making bookshelves?''

''Nothing at all,'' Oscar said. ''But Grandfather wouldn't have brought this wood into the house. It would have been oak for him, properly seasoned, perhaps from a tree he'd felled himself. Then he'd have looked at it for a bit, deciding which surfaces he'd show, for the look of the grain, for the appearance of the finished piece. Oh, he would have taken his time over that. And he wouldn't have screwed it together, as we shall, and braced it. No, he'd have used his sharp little saw and the whole thing would have been fitted together with mortice and tenon joints, every one of them identical, perfect. Then glued and clamped. And every corner would have been true. The shelves would last longer than the house.''

''Would you like to do that sort of work?'' I said. I had the idea of commissioning some piece of furniture, a chest maybe, or a tallboy, and allowing Oscar to work with love and pride, like his grandfather.

''Not me,'' he said. ''We haven't time for such things. Your shelves will hold books as well as any my grandfather made. And we'll finish them today. They'll be standing in your room tonight. My old lad would have taken a week.''

He stood up and brushed the crumbs from the front of his red shirt.

''We are different people,'' he said, ''living in a different world. What's the point of using skills no longer necessary? What's the point of dreaming of a world full of archangel? There isn't any. We have to use what's left. When there isn't any timber left, we'll find something else.''

161

We picked up one of the long side panels and began to measure it for the fitting which would enable me to adapt the widths between the shelves.

"How long has the old man been dead?" I asked. I was interested in him.

"Fifteen years," Oscar said. "He died fifteen years last February."

I held the wood while he drilled the small holes for the bronze screws we were going to use.

"I was working at Horsham at the time," he said, "on that estate the other side of the railway station. Nice houses, good quality. I was living there then, in Horsham, not long married, about eighteen months."

We put down the plank and picked up the next.

"My mother telephoned the site office and asked the foreman to let me know the old chap was dead. I came down that afternoon. He'd left me his house, tools, furniture, everything. Well, I was always with him, and I was the only grandson. I'd looked after his garden for years, since I was big enough. His chickens, rabbits. I just stepped right back as if I'd never been away."

"I didn't know you'd ever left here," I said. "I always think of you as part of this place, like the trees and houses."

"I've been about," Oscar said. "I served my apprenticeship with a big firm, worked in Bristol for a few weeks once, was in Leeds, Birmingham. I was quite a while in Birmingham. It was a good firm. They wanted me to stay when I'd worked my time, but I'd rather work on my own. I came back, worked here and there, never very far away. I was married when I was twenty."

"You surprise me, Oscar," I said. "Why haven't you told me this before?"

"We never got round to it," he said. "It was talking about old Ted Armitage that brought it on now, I suppose. And I didn't think you'd be interested. I think of your mind full of bookshelves as far as the eye can see, with the files of books waiting for you to use."

He grinned at me.

"I've lived here ever since the old man died," he said. "It was as if he knew something was wanted, something needed doing. We were up there in Horsham and we'd just lost our first baby, Enid and I. A little girl, lovely little thing. I was astonished when I first saw her, such small hands. She was holding them up to her mouth, and waving them now and then."

"What happened?" I said.

"When she was four months old," Oscar said, "she died in her cot. She hadn't been ill. Nobody could explain it. It happens sometimes, everybody told us."

He stopped drilling and lifted the wood to his eye, judging its accuracy.

"But it was obviously time for a new start," he said. "We had to put things behind us. After we buried my grandfather we moved straight into his house and we've lived there ever since."

"I'm sorry," I said, "about your baby."

"Over and done with," he said. "It's not often I think of it. Enid does, I know; but what is gone, is gone. There's no sense in wishing for things past. There's no sense in hoping for things to come back."

We'd finished the shelves by the end of the afternoon. I wasn't going to have them stained or polished in any way, just the plain, smooth wood. Oscar approved of this.

"They look a bit raw and new," he said, "but they'll darken. As you use them they'll acquire a few marks here and there, become yours, get a bit of character."

We piled his folding workbench and the tools into his truck, and I paid him.

"Want some plums?" he said, tucking the money into his pocket. "We've a huge crop of Victorias, far too many for us."

It's sensible to accept what Oscar offers. He gives generously and proudly, a proud man, fiercely independent.

"I'd like that," I said, "I'm fond of plums."

"Follow me down, then," he said, "and bring a basket."

Oscar's two little boys were in the garden when we arrived and they helped me to fill my shallow basket with purple Victoria plums, an old sort from an old tree, lush and full, the flawless bloom on them. I got in the car to drive away and all three stood to watch me go, their attitudes identical, the same smiles, their feet turned out in the same way. Oscar put his arms around his sons.

"Who needs archangel?" he said.

That night I filled my new bookshelves, sorting the books and arranging them carefully, watching them bring the room to life. It was a splendid thing to be doing. I enjoyed doing it.

Leslie Norris's many works include *Walking the White Fields: Poems 1967-80*; *Selected Poems* (1986); *Sequences* (1988); *Sliding* (1986), a collection of stories for which he received the triannually awarded international Katherine Mansfield Award in Fiction and the David Higham Memorial Prize; and *Norris's Ark*, a collection of his children's verse. A frequent contributor to the *Atlantic* and the *New Yorker*, Norris has taught at a number of universities in England and America, and was a Theodore Roethke Lecturer at the University of Washington.

Leslie Norris was born in Merthyr Tydfil, Wales, and educated there and at the University of Southampton. As a teacher and writer he has lived in England, Wales, and Washington. He currently lives in Utah and is a Professor of English at Brigham Young University, where his wife, Kitty, also teaches.